# Blame it on Lord Raine

The Three Graces
Book 3

*Alanna Lucas*

## ARE YOU SIGNED UP FOR DRAGONBLADE'S BLOG?

You'll get the latest news and information on exclusive giveaways, exclusive excerpts, coming releases, sales, free books, cover reveals and more.

Check out our complete list of authors, too!

No spam, no junk. That's a promise!

### Sign Up Here

www.dragonbladepublishing.com

*Dearest Reader;*

*Thank you for your support of a small press. At Dragonblade Publishing, we strive to bring you the highest quality Historical Romance from some of the best authors in the business. Without your support, there is no 'us', so we sincerely hope you adore these stories and find some new favorite authors along the way.*

*Happy Reading!*

*CEO, Dragonblade Publishing*

# Additional Dragonblade books by Author Alanna Lucas

**The Three Graces Series**
A Most Improper Duchess (Book 1)
Never Judge a Beast by His Cover (Book 2)
Blame it on Lord Raine (Book 3)

**The Lyon's Den Series**
How to Steal a Lyon's Fortune

# Chapter One

*Grimsby Hall, Summer 1817*

"So, WE MEET again," Lord Raine said with suave confidence, startling her as she stormed into the parlor.

"Argh!" Evelina exasperated.

Evelina eyed the rake with what she hoped was intense disdain. All she wanted was a moment alone to ease her nerves after *his* surprise arrival this evening, and he was in the one room she'd chosen for her refuge. *Why was he even here?*

Before she could stop the words, she spewed, "Why in the hell are you here?"

He pushed off the wall and began to saunter toward her. "Such language for a proper miss." His deep and seductive tone sent a warm ripple down her spine, settling in places too intimate to name. *Damn him.*

Crossing her arms, she attempted to keep her wits about her. It was quite difficult what with the way his chocolate-brown eyes moved along her body, taking in every inch of her. She swallowed hard, fighting the effects of his attention. *He is a rake. He is a seducer of women. He is . . .*

*Getting far too close.*

"Lord Raine," she began to say as she backed away toward the door. She had to make her escape before anyone discovered she was alone with a rake. "I do not intend to have a verbal sparring match with you. Whatever the reason you have decided to intrude on this country house party is your affair and does not concern me." Two more steps and she would be safe.

In two strides, Lord Raine was at her side, a breath away, but he did not touch her. Her first mistake was looking up into his handsome visage. Her second was licking her lips. His eyes flared with a hunger that was pure desire, making her knees wobble. *He's a rake. Do not let him affect you. Rakes are nothing but trouble and will only cause heartache.*

"Oh, it does concern you, Sweetness."

Voices drifted in from down the hall, and just as swiftly as he had been at her side, he turned and dashed from the room, leaving her alone and, thankfully, untouched.

What was it about that man that raised her heartbeat and made her want to slap him hard against the face? No, not slap, but punch. And not just hard, but very hard.

"Oh, there you are," Theodora said as she entered the room. Her younger sister narrowed her gaze, inspecting her. "Is anything the matter?"

"Nothing that can be discussed at present." Her response brought a gasp from Theodora, and Evelina quickly added, "Nothing untoward, I just don't want anyone to jump to conclusions."

Theodora then whispered, "Lord Raine?"

In a firm, hushed tone, Evelina pointed her finger at her sister and said, "You are not to say *his* name."

"Yes. I forgot," the words dripped with sarcasm.

"I'm sorry." She went to her sister's side. "I don't know why *he* annoys me so, but—"

"Perhaps it is not annoyance you're feeling when he's around. Perhaps it is—"

"Theodora Hera Grace, do not say what I think you're going to, and certainly do *not* think it! He is the last man I would ever consider marrying. He is a rake and a scoundrel and altogether unsuitable."

Theodora's auburn brow raised in suspicion. "Sounds like a lot of protests."

*It did.* But it was true. Evelina was not interested in the attentions of a rake, and a scoundrel could not possibly make a good husband. Oh, to be sure, he was handsome and tall, and when he walked into a room, one could not help but notice him and stare. And then there was his deep seductive voice that sent warmth throughout her body, and . . . *stop that!*

Evelina would not fall victim to his charms, and that was that. She sucked in a deep breath and, on a long slow exhale that did not ease her nerves, said, "Shall we rejoin the others and enjoy what remains of the evening?"

"I suppose. But," Theodora emphasized the word, sounding more like an overly protective mother than a younger sister, "We *will* discuss this later."

"Yes, Theodora."

HOURS LATER, EVERYONE had retired—everyone, save Evelina and Theodora. Sitting on her comfortable bed, Evelina began to recount the events from earlier in the evening. With every word she spoke, her nerves became more tightly wound. *Why did he continue to torment her?*

"And what exactly did you say to him?" Her sister's question brought her out of her distressed thoughts.

"I asked him why he was here."

"Lord—" Theodora stopped short from saying *his* name, then continued in an apologetic tone, *"He's* here because his sister is."

"Then why did he not just say so when I asked him?" She had been irked by his cool, debonair manner, and it had not subsided with time.

"I don't know. What else did he say?"

"He didn't answer the question. Then I told him that him being here did not concern me, and then he said that it does and he called me *Sweetness*." Evelina knew she was rambling, but she hoped her sentences were at least coherent. Though she could never be certain, because whenever she thought of *him* or spoke about *him*, her mind was muddled and confused.

"Sweetness?" Theodora's mouth opened wide on a gasp. "Perhaps he wants to have his way with you?"

"Be serious," she said as she crossed her arms. "He's a rake, and I have not once swooned at the sight of him. I think he's just trying to get a rise out of me."

"But why? In London, he accused *you* of trying to seduce *him*. Now, he shows up to a country house party and says you're the reason he's here." Theodora thought for a moment, then offered, "Perhaps Miss Raine knows his purpose in behaving this way?"

"Do you really believe he would tell his sister what his motives are?"

"No, but remember, Miss Raine told us she likes to eavesdrop on her brother. Maybe she's heard something? And if she hasn't, perhaps she would be willing to aid us." Theodora was clearly in a plotting mood.

"I don't want to raise her alarm. Miss Raine has enough to contend with, what with her miserable aunt chaperoning her."

"True," Theodora agreed, then added, "We can make something up about some other lady . . . someone we met in London. We won't tell Miss Raine her name. We'll say it is to protect the lady's identity."

"Do you really believe that excuse will work?" Evelina said. Ladies had been searching out the Grace sisters and their salon for advice since the beginning of last Season. It seemed rather odd to reverse the role now, even in such a guise as this.

Theodora grinned. "Yes. Miss Raine told me she has been anxious to use her eavesdropping skills for the good of our salon. We might as well use that to our advantage."

Evelina still wasn't certain it would work, but it was worth a try. It was not as if they'd come up with any better ideas. And she certainly would not rest well with that scoundrel present.

THE FOOD WAS delicious, but dinner had passed in painfully slow measures as Evelina counted the minutes until the moment when she and Theodora would be able to speak with Miss Raine.

And although they sat at opposite ends of the table, she could feel *his* heated gaze on her the entire time. Throughout the meal, she kept shifting in her seat, wondering how much more of this she could endure.

What felt like hours later, dinner had concluded, and the opportunity to speak to Miss Raine finally presented itself. With the gentlemen taking their brandy, it was the perfect time for the sisters to question Miss Raine without *his* piercing gaze disrupting Evelina's thoughts, her entire being really. *Oh, that odious man!*

As the ladies entered the drawing room, Evelina and Theodora decided on which part of the room would allow for the most privacy—as if privacy were truly an option in a room of chatty women. Hopefully, the conversations of others would mask their own.

"No one is seated near the large tapestry at the far end," Theodora said under her breath as she shifted her eyes in the direction indicated.

Evelina quickly glanced to where Theodora suggested. "That is a perfect location. We could ask her to take a turn about the room and then casually stop in front of the tapestry."

The sisters nodded in agreement and then, with their plan in place, went to where Miss Raine was standing with Mrs. Raine and Lady Gordon.

"Would you care to take a turn about the room?" Theodora asked with a sweet smile that was meant to soften the stern resolve of the older women present.

"That would be lovely, especially after sitting for so long," Miss Raine said as she moved away from her chaperone and Lady Gordon, not giving them the opportunity to object. The trio began to stroll the length of the long drawing room in silence. Once clear of the other guests, Daisy whispered, "Thank you for rescuing me. My aunt has been nigh impossible with her persistence that Lord Neave would make an excellent match. She's even enlisted Lady Gordon to help sway my mind."

Evelina thought the man very kind and sincere. In her estimation, Miss Raine could do far worse, and she came to the gentleman's defense. "Lord Neave is not an unpleasant fellow."

"No, of course he's not, and I meant nothing ill against him, but I have my cap set at another." She then added in a barely audible tone, "I think that is why my brother has arrived."

Evelina glanced to Theodora who met her gaze. This was the information they were hoping for, and offered without their thin pretense.

Theodora asked the question that was on both their minds. "He does not approve of the gentleman you're interested in?"

Miss Raine glanced about, ensuring no one was paying heed to their conversation. "He doesn't know who it is."

"Then how do you know he is here for that reason?" Evelina questioned, hoping for understanding, although the way the conversation was progressing with Miss Raine's increasingly ungrounded speculations, she was beginning to wonder if she would obtain the answers she sought.

"Why else *would* he be here?" Daisy asked with a shrug of her shoulders. "Ever since Mrs. Fleming's dinner party in Town, he's been far too interested in the company I keep. He is always interfering, asking me questions about who I spend my time with and whether he is ever mentioned in conversation. I overheard him tell our cousin that women like to seduce rakes for the fun of it. What nonsense. I highly doubt anyone is trying to seduce him." She shook her head and added in a sarcastic tone, "And besides, my brother is not that interesting, I assure you."

Alarm bells rang in Evelina's head. She had been at that dinner party and had an encounter with Lord Raine that evening during which he accused her of following him, tempting him at

6

every turn, *and* trying to seduce him. What sort of game was he playing?

Evelina was still trying to comprehend Lord Raine's motives when her sister—who thankfully still had her wits about her—inquired, "How long is Lord Raine expected to be a guest here?"

"Only a couple of days. He is to visit with our uncle and his family before traveling to Bath to see Mother, and he knows better than to delay a visit with her."

*I can survive two days.*

Two days had passed. It was the longest two days of her life, but finally Lord Raine was gone. She was exhausted from trying to avoid him. It seemed as if every time she'd turned around, *he* was there. Despite him taking his leave of the country house party, she suspected it was not the last she would see of him. She and Theodora still had not come up with a reasonable explanation as to why he had come in the first place. Both sisters agreed that it likely had little to do with his sister. Theodora even had the audacity to suggest *he* had formed a tendre for her. And if that claim was not outrageous enough, her younger sister then added insult to injury and stated that she believed that Evelina had formed one for the very man she'd been trying to avoid!

It was too completely preposterous to even consider!

But Evelina was not going to think about his motives at the moment. She was simply going to enjoy the rest of the house party with her sister and friends. If her suspicions were correct, Theodora herself had formed a tendre for Lord Grimsby.

Sadness and longing squeezed her heart.

She was so happy for both her sisters, but it was all changing. The life she'd lived with her parents and siblings was becoming a distant memory. What did her own future hold?

# Chapter Two

*London, two weeks later*

J AMES' MOTHER STORMED into his study as if her lecture earlier in
the day regarding his sister's elopement with Mr. Douglas
Malone had not already been sufficient. No, she needed to
readdress *The Scandal of the Year* as she so firmly put it.

Was he ever to complete his tasks? The pile of things he
needed to do was growing by the hour, and yet he had not a
moment of privacy to get even one item done.

He didn't look up from the ledger as he began to remind his
mother, "The outcome has not changed—" he began but was
interrupted.

She threw up her hands and demanded in a loud voice that
reverberated through the room, "There must be something that
can be done, or rather undone. I cannot go out in Society with
the scandal marring our family's reputation."

Pushing the more pressing obligation aside, he attempted to
reason with her. "Mother, would you please calm yourself—"

"I do not need to calm *myself.*" The moment she took in a
deep breath, he knew another lecture was forthcoming. "You
need to act on behalf of this family. *You* let this happen. What do
*you* intend to do about your sister?"

"It's not as if she married a farmer. She married the son of a
viscount. I'm a viscount, so you—"

"She married a *third* son of a viscount. That is quite different."
She pointed a firm and angry finger at him. "And you know it."

"Not every lady can be expected to marry the firstborn son and—"

Once again reason fell on deaf ears.

"I expected *my* daughter to marry a firstborn son. There is no excuse or reason for why she did not."

James knew the reason, but also knew his mother would not hear any of it. By the time he'd learned of Daisy's plans and caught up with the pair, they had already married and consummated the union. He'd had no choice but to accept Mr. Malone into their family in order to keep further gossip at bay. Daisy was adamant that she'd married for love, that all she desired was to spend her life with her darling Douglas. In turn, Mr. Malone had assured James that he would devote his entire life to making *his* Daisy happy. It was a beautiful sentiment and one James knew he was incapable of having. He wasn't sure love even existed. Lust and desire, yes. But love? No. Not in his family at least.

*Perhaps it would be different for Daisy.*

"Mother, please—"

"No," she said with a stomp of a firm foot. "And do you know who is to blame?" His stomach knotted, and he held his breath as he waited for her to say his name. Since his father had died, it was always thus. He was always at fault for whatever went wrong in his mother's eyes. "Those Grace sisters. They had something to do with it, I just know it. Especially the middle one. Miss Evelina Grace is nothing but trouble."

He was shocked that his mother hadn't said his name, but even more so when she laid the blame at Evelina's feet. Evelina and Miss Theodora *had* been present at Lord Grimsby's house party. Would Evelina go as far to aid his sister in scandal just because of her dislike of him?

Without a doubt, he knew the answer to be yes. But knowing she *would* and knowing she *had* were two different things. However, the Grace sisters *were* somewhat notorious for having aided their friends in the past over the objections of their families. Rumors swirled that the sisters aided Lady Naomi in her elopement, but . . .

"Oh, why do such unfortunate things always happen to me? *You* have to fix this! What am I to do?" she wailed. "You do realize I cannot attend Lady Holland's ball this evening." Mother put a dramatic hand to her forehead. "Can you imagine the gossip and whispers I would have to endure?"

"Then just stay in tonight, Mother," he snapped, not knowing what else to say that would appease his mother. He was at his wits' end with all her dramatics.

Eyes wide with shock, she huffed, then with another stomp of her foot, left the room, lecturing to the air since surely no one else was listening to her tirade.

James didn't know how but, somehow, he would fix the situation and squelch the rumors.

HOURS LATER, HIS temper was at a boiling point. His mother had spent the remainder of the afternoon and the early evening taking every opportunity to demand his action while simultaneously preventing him from attending to estate business. He finally went to his club, hoping to find peace in a drink, but the moment he encountered Lord Sparling, what little calm he had left quickly disappeared.

"I hear that your sister ran off with Lord Malone's youngest?" Lord Sparling said with a chuckle as he took the seat beside James.

"I don't remember inviting you to sit with me," James snarled. He was not in the mood this evening to deal with this pompous ass.

Sparling inspected his hand as he spoke. "I meant nothing ill by it, just thought you'd be interested in some fascinating information Lord Jerome revealed to me earlier."

Lord Jerome's wife was a notorious gossip who made it her business to know *everyone's* business. Through the years, Lady Jerome had caused more harm to reputations than he could remember. However, it was never good to cross her or be on her bad side.

"In case you're wondering," Lord Sparling started, then paused, waiting for James to meet his gaze. "It has to do with your sister and her connection to a certain salon."

*The Three Graces Salon.*

All last Season, he'd heard gossip about their goings-on but he dismissed those rumors as utter nonsense. Surely Lady Middleton would have never allowed her great-nieces to hold such an inappropriate salon under her care. Or, a more likely reason, she hadn't known.

Lord Sparling was a snake. He didn't trust the man, but James wanted answers and Lord Sparling seemed ready to provide them. He would listen, then decide the next course of action. James offered a nod, encouraging the man to talk.

Before he spilled the tale, Sparling said, "Consider this information proof of my friendship to your family." James did not respond, but narrowed his gaze and stared the man down, waiting for him to elaborate. "It would seem your sister has been spending considerable time with a certain group of ladies. And they are the ones who helped arrange for your sister's elopement while at Grimsby's house party. It was all planned right under your poor aunt's nose."

James had no trouble believing his aunt would tell Lady Jerome her sad tale. Ever since the elopement, she'd fallen out of his mother's good graces and was most desperate to be reinstated within the folds of the family.

James was about to ask which ladies Lord Sparling was referring to when the man leaned in and said, "In case you're wondering who the ladies were, look no further than the salon-hosting Grace sisters."

*Evelina Grace.*

All the suspicions and presumptions he'd had about her suddenly came into focus. James was right to believe she could be an accomplice. He *knew* Evelina Grace to be nothing but trouble. Why else had she been disrupting his thoughts all these months? "Good night," he growled as he stood and took his leave of Lord Sparling. He had much to contemplate.

AFTER LEARNING THAT Miss Grace was due to be at Lady Holland's ball that evening, he changed his clothes and went straight there. He did not know what he would do or say when he finally met Miss Grace again, but one thing was for certain, she would have a great deal to explain.

But an hour into the ball, James still had not spotted the infuriating woman and was growing impatient. He did not want to be at Lady Holland's ball. He did not want to dance. He did not want to socialize.

What he did want was revenge.

What gave Miss Evelina Grace the authority to encourage his sister to elope to Gretna Green with Mr. Douglas Malone? Matters were settled with his sister, but he was still fuming over Evelina's audacity in aiding his innocent little sister.

*Is that truly why you are angry?*

*Of course*, he argued with himself. *Why else?*

Just then, a lush feminine figure in pale green with silky auburn hair caught his attention from across the room. *Evelina.*

He watched her interact with two young ladies and couldn't help but wonder if she was aiding them in some nefarious quest as well. Although the other chits looked enthralled with all that surrounded them, the auburn-haired beauty seemed distracted, almost distraught. And then her gaze turned, and for the briefest of seconds, their eyes met. James was entranced. What was it about Evelina that always made his heart skip a beat? He'd been with plenty of women, and none had ever affected him the way this one provocative woman had. He had the strongest, strangest urge to make Evelina his, and not just for a night, or even a Season. And he most certainly did not want her in the arms of another.

In the next moment, she broke eye contact, turned, and briskly walked away, heading toward the veranda. He didn't know what came over him, but his initial reason for wanting to see her vanished as he moved toward her, guided by an invincible force.

As he stepped onto the veranda, he saw her standing alone at the edge, looking out onto the moon-washed landscape. No sooner had he taken another step, than she whipped around.

"Why are you following me, Lord Raine?"

The reason he was here came back full force and punched him in the gut. *Daisy.* "I want to know who gave you the authority to aid my sister in eloping with Mr. Malone."

"Someone with some common sense needed to step in and aid her or she would have found herself arranged to be married to one of the men of Mrs. Raine's choosing. Your aunt is far too judgmental and only concerned with herself. Mr. Malone comes from a good family—"

His temper was rising with each breath he took. "He's a third son . . ." Good Lord, he sounded like his mother. The thought soured in his stomach. He did not want to be like either of his parents.

"So, you would keep them apart because *you* believe he is not worthy?" She then threw his words back at him. "Who gave *you* the authority to keep two people in love apart?"

He could not hide his disdain for the word. "In *love?* You believe them to be in love?"

She let out a contemptuous laugh that struck a nerve.

James stepped closer to her. "Why do you laugh?" the words rumbled from his mouth.

"I'm not surprised you do not believe in love and—"

One moment she was reprimanding him, telling him what

she thought of him, and in the next, James had pulled Evelina into an embrace and was kissing her as if she were the only woman in the world who mattered.

EVELINA DID NOT know how she went from arguing with Lord Raine to being kissed by him. A deep intoxicating kiss that made her toes curl as desire like she'd never felt before filled her body, demanding more, wanting more of his touch, wanting . . .

*Oh no! She was being kissed by the very rake she'd been trying to avoid!*

Dawning realization slapped her across the face as she pushed away from Lord Raine, but it was too late. Even in the moonlight she could see the shocked faces of nearly a dozen people staring at her from the doorway back into the ballroom. Then a moment later, her world turned upside down as one of the onlookers pushed through the crowd.

"Miss Grace!" a single voice broke through the haze of desire and confusion. *Miss Jerome.* She was second only to her mother, Lady Jerome, as the worst gossipmonger Evelina had ever had the displeasure of meeting. Miss Jerome had been spreading tittle-tattle about Evelina and her sisters since their first Season.

Lord Raine backed away and glanced around at those on the veranda, then his eyes settled on Evelina. "We will marry," was all he said before he pushed though the curious onlookers and walked away.

*We will marry?* Rage and anger flared through her body as his declaration settled into the pit of her stomach. How could this have occurred?

"Evelina," Aunt Imogene started as she rushed to her side, "What just happened?"

As much as Evelina wanted to be comforted by her dearest aunt, her desire to leave posthaste was far greater. She shook her head and whispered, "I should like to return home now."

Only a short time later, Evelina and her aunt were back at their home, but she did not feel any relief. Her thoughts and emotions over what had just happened and their implications roiled through her until they lost all meaning. Fortunately, her aunt did not press for answers, and instead, consoled her with loving care.

Trying to ease Evelina's worries, Aunt Imogene tried to reassure her that all would turn out well in the end, and that nothing else could be done at the moment, except to wait for her brother to come to Town. Evelina did not know how Harold would handle what was set to become a full-blown scandal. It was not as if he'd shown any interest in her or sisters in years. Dozens of scenarios pounded against her temples. *Damn, what am I to do?*

There was only one option. All she could do was wait until Harold arrived and weigh possible next steps once she knew his reaction.

So. She'd wait and fester over what was to happen next. She'd just experienced the most thrilling kiss of her life *and* the rogue who kissed her declared in front of dozens that they would marry! Damn *him*! Why did *he* have to stir such excitement within, *and* be the one man who shouldn't?

She had to find a way out. She had not only vowed to only marry for love—and she certainly did not hold that affection for the rogue—but also to never succumb to rakes. And that especially included James.

No. Lord Raine.

No. *Him.* She vowed to never succumb to *him.*

Oh, but that kiss and how it sent such ripples of pleasure surging through her, and the pull she felt whenever he was near . . .

*Stop that!*

She must push those pesky, unbidden feelings of attraction she had toward him as far away as possible. She absolutely must.

*Never be afraid of desire.* Her late, beloved mother's words suddenly echoed in her mind. She certainly felt that for *him.* But

Mother also said that her own greatest desire was for her daughters to find a love and friendship like she'd had with their father. Love and friendship were not synonymous with Lord Raine . . . no, *him*.

Evelina must find a way out of this.

# Chapter Three

T HE ONLY REASON James was not concerned about this meeting with Evelina's brother was that he knew Lord Grace would not call him out. Lord Grace was known as a notoriously bad shot, and since his marriage, he'd lost any other semblance of manhood as well.

James, on the other hand, was an excellent shot, swift with his fists, and a practiced swordsman. Not that he felt the need to boast about his qualities, but Lord Grace would indeed be a fool to challenge him. And besides, James was not entirely upset with the turn of events.

For months, all he'd dreamt about, desired, was Evelina, which probably was the driving force in his impulsive actions at Lady Holland's ball. But now was as good a time as any to settle down, so why not do so with a woman as beautiful and well-born as Evelina? Not to mention his desire for an heir.

As James walked into Lord Grace's London study, he could not help but notice how altered the once-vibrant man looked. His dark brown hair was streaked with thick strands of grey, his face tired and sagging. James suspected his present countenance had more to do with his wife than the current scandal with his sister.

He took a seat across from Lord Grace and waited.

"Thank you for responding so promptly to my request." Lord

Grace ran a trembling hand through his already tousled hair. "Dammit, I knew this day would come. Evelina has always been rather headstrong." He shook his head and sighed deeply as if he were most distressed over this situation. James suspected otherwise. James had heard enough rumors over the years regarding the Graces' marital status that made his own parents' marriage seem pleasant at times. If anything, the spineless lord was more likely distressed over having to listen to his wife berate him over his sister's behavior. "I will get straight to the point. I will not support a ruined spinster. As much as it pains me, and since I have no choice, I will honor her dowry, and you will marry her."

James knew this was as close as Lord Grace would come to calling him out. Not only did he not care for Harold's implied threat, he did not care for the way he spoke about his own sister. Although James did not always get on well with his own sisters, he'd always tried to act in their best interests. He had every intention of marrying the delectable Evelina, but just the same, he would not take orders from this man.

"I do not take well to threats. I *will* marry Evelina because I *want* to marry her."

Relief eased the worry lines around Lord Grace's eyes. "Since you want to marry her, I assume you will have a proper wedding with the reading of the banns?"

James suspected the request was in reference to Evelina's two sisters who'd both married quickly by special license, stirring gossip over possible scandals in the process. But he would not give Lord Grace the satisfaction of dictating any course of action chosen to begin his and *his* future bride's life together.

"No," he began firmly, "We will marry by special license."

Lord Grace looked as if to argue, but no opposition was forthcoming. He then placed both hands on the desk, stood, and sighed, worry lines crinkling his features once again. "I will inform my wife. You may inform Evelina. I wish you both well."

And with that, James took his leave, his next destination clear in his mind.

EVELINA WAS ENJOYING the quiet afternoon in the sunlit parlor, but she knew it wouldn't last. At any moment, she feared Harold would arrive at Aunt Imogene's home and demand she marry Lord Raine. Of all his possible reactions to the situation, this seemed the most likely. She'd prepared a speech, hoping to be spared the unwanted marriage. It wasn't her fault Lord Raine had kissed her, so why then should she be made to suffer? For months, she'd been trying to avoid his presence, and for months, he'd shown up at every event. No, if anyone deserved to suffer, it was him.

She was hoping to convince her brother to allow her to retreat to the country with Aunt Imogene while the gossip died down and then reenter Society in a year or two. The longer the better. She was tired of the *ton* and the marriage mart game. Time in the country to enjoy the simpler pleasures of life, read poetry, perhaps even write some verses herself—that was just what she needed. And surely, over time, the gossip would fade, wouldn't it? At the very least, both her sisters were happily married and would, hopefully, be untouched by the scandal she'd—no, *he'd*—created.

Just then, Roger—Aunt Imogene's butler—entered the room, interrupting her dream. *Harold had arrived.* She stood and smoothed her damp hands down the front of her dress, readying for battle.

"Lord Raine is here to see you, miss," the longtime butler announced with a sympathetic tone, then took his leave.

*Lord Raine?*

A moment later, the last man she wanted to see strolled into the room with all the confidence of a Greek god. He was too handsome by far with his strong jaw, deep brown eyes, honey blond hair, and devil may care attitude.

Evelina opened her mouth, about to put him in his place,

when Lord Raine spoke, "I come in peace." He almost sounded sincere, but she knew better.

"Peace?" she said with a cynical laugh. She had not been truly at peace since before she'd first met him all those months ago. And she was just about to say as much when he interrupted her thoughts.

"I've spoken with your brother, and he has consented to our marriage. He wishes us well."

"Harold is not coming?" The words tore from her lips. She was more surprised, she supposed, than she ought to be. He hadn't taken much interest in any of his sisters' lives since his marriage to Rachel, but it stung just the same. "What did he say? Exactly." She deserved the truth.

"He said he would not support a spinster and expects us to marry."

She looked into Lord Raine's eyes, assessing whether he was lying but all she saw was sympathy, and something deeper that she couldn't quite understand. A surge of emotions stormed her insides. Emotions she did not want to contemplate. All she was certain of at that moment was that she didn't want to be forced into marriage, but without any support from her brother she had few choices left. *Damn Society and all its absurd rules!* Perhaps she could strike a bargain with Lord Raine. But what sort of—

"If we do not marry," his words broke through her internal ramblings, only adding to her dread, "you will have no income." Lord Raine took a step closer, never breaking eye contact. "We will marry by special license in three days' time."

She gulped hard and fought back the tears. "Three days?"

How would she survive this? How would she survive without it? She knew Aunt Imogene and her sisters would gladly take her in, but she did not want to be a burden on them. And even if they did, with the scandal marring her name, her future prospects would certainly be limited.

Although . . . if a gentleman *did* want to marry her in spite of everything, it would certainly be a love match, wouldn't it?

*Perhaps it wouldn't.* Perhaps she'd find herself in a worse situation. A situation where some other future husband may only want to use her for her dowry or her connections within the *ton*. After all, one of her sisters had married a duke and the other an earl.

How could she have allowed herself to get into this situation? This was exactly what she and her sisters had been trying to avoid with the creation of their salon, and she'd fallen right into the rake's trap.

Steaming heat rose up from within, disintegrating any possibility for future happiness. What other choice did she truly have in the end?

Evelina nodded her head in acceptance but kept the anger simmering inside her to herself. There was nothing she could do without ruining herself. She would retain her dignity if nothing else. The gossips would have a field day if she did not go through with this wedding. And then what would her life hold?

"That should allow plenty of time for your sisters to arrive and—"

She raised her chin and with all the defiance she could muster, informed him, "I will not be inviting them."

How could she? True, they were not only her sisters, but also her dearest friends, and she never kept anything from them for very long, but how would she ever explain this?

Alexandra and Theodora both had married for love and expected Evelina to do the same. She could not possibly tell them the truth. Not yet. She was too humiliated, embarrassed, and altogether out of sorts. Once she was married, she would send a letter to her sisters, explaining what had occurred.

He interrupted her dire musings, clearly losing his patience as he argued, "How would it look if none of your family were present?"

"Aunt Imogene will be there to help *celebrate* this *joyful* occasion." She hoped he heard the sarcasm dripping with each word loud and clear.

"The Duke and Duchess of Blackburn, and Lord and Lady

Grimsby *will* be invited," Lord Raine said with a firmness that insinuated she was not to argue. He was about to learn otherwise.

*If* her family were to be present and *if* she had to enter into a loveless marriage, the least she could do was benefit from his insistence.

She crossed her arms and stood her ground. "Fine. Although I understand that this union is a necessity, and since it is you, Lord Raine, who is to blame for that necessity, there are things that I require."

Through gritted teeth, he replied, "Such as?"

"Freedom to host ladies of the *ton*, to spend time in the country—without your interreference—and to keep my dowry for my future use alone. And in return, I will be a perfect viscountess, hosting soirées and dinner parties."

He was silent for a moment, clearly contemplating her demands. She braced herself for an argument. "I agree on one condition." She was taken aback that he did not argue, but she suspected the battle had only just begun.

"And what might that be?"

"I require an heir."

*An heir.* That meant that they would have to . . .

Her world tilted on its side as thoughts of being intimate with James—*no, him*—warmed her insides before searing heat flared.

Evelina would not bring a baby into a loveless marriage. It didn't matter if that was the way of the *ton*, it was not her way. She squared her shoulders, lifted her chin, and once again with as much defiance as she could muster, stated, "And I require love." She held his gaze, determined not to back down. Seconds passed and when he did not respond, she added, "It looks like neither of us will get what we truly desire."

She did not wait for him to respond, but simply turned and strolled from the room.

*Three days later*

EVELINA STOOD IN front of the mirror, eyeing her reflection, wondering exactly how she'd landed herself in this predicament. Both her sisters had married for love and here she was, not even marrying for like. Over the past days, she'd considered running away, but then what? It wasn't in her nature to run away. That seemed far too dramatic, even for her.

Even though the kiss and current predicament weren't her doing, Evelina was too embarrassed by the turn of events. *You're not completely innocent in this game*, she reminded herself. She inwardly shook her head, not wanting to admit that she had courted scandal ever since that first night she encountered Lord Raine, and it only escalated at Mrs. Fleming's dinner party. She'd been far too bold in informing him that if she *were* trying to seduce him, she would not be coy about it, but perform a bold act. Every time she'd seen him, been near him, all caution flew away in a gale. What was it about *him* that drove her to extremes?

Before she could consider an answer, a soft *knock knock* sounded on the door, then it opened and two of the sweetest faces she dearly adored entered the room.

"Alexandra, Theodora," she cried as her sisters rushed into the room and into each other's arms. Being within her sisters' embrace eased some of the anxiety she'd been experiencing.

"I've missed you so much," Alexandra said as she squeezed both sisters, then kissed each of their cheeks.

"It feels like it's been years since the three of us were together," Theodora said with a sniffle, clearly fighting back tears.

She missed being with her sisters more than she could ever express. *Don't cry*, she begged herself. Although she knew she'd been wrong to try and keep them away, Evelina also was not prepared to reveal all her feelings about . . . well, everything. Besides, what could she say when she didn't know what exactly she *was* feeling? Evelina felt as if she were trapped between obligation and duty, want and desire, and not knowing exactly what she wanted.

Alexandra released the sisters, then took a step back. "I just knew there was more than met the eye with the two of you."

"Me, too," Theodora agreed. "Especially after he showed up at Damian's house party. I knew he was there to see you."

"Yes, and the constant insistence that we not say *his* name, or the subtle flirting that passed between you two," Alexandra said with a teasing smile.

Evelina stood speechless, too discomposed about what she was hearing and feeling to argue. She'd never given *him* any indication that she would accept his advances. Or had she?

No. She knew her sisters to be wrong, but she was prepared to let them believe it was a happy union, if for nothing else, to not cause them anxiety. After all, she'd already resolved that she had no other option than to go through with the marriage. Dear as her sisters were, what more could they do but worry?

Her eldest and youngest sister stood back and eyed her, as if they knew something she did not. Why couldn't they just tell her and be done with it? She was wrestling with saying as much when her eldest sister took a step closer.

"You look beautiful, dearest," Alexandra said as she rubbed a gentle finger across the cameo at Evelina's neck. "So much like Mother." She kissed Evelina's cheek, then whispered, "I know you will be most happy."

Evelina swallowed the hard lump in her throat and simply smiled. There was nothing else she could say at the moment without revealing all the turmoil within. She felt as if her heart was breaking.

"It's time," Aunt Imogene said she entered into the room. "Oh, you three look lovely together. I only wish your mother were here to see you together. She would have been so proud of her three girls." The pride that reverberated in her words sealed Evelina's fate. She would never reveal her true emotions and would simply endure a loveless marriage.

Perhaps it wouldn't be too awful.

# Chapter Four

A s Evelina stepped from the carriage—followed by her sisters and great-aunt—a crisp chill wisped past them, reflecting the arrangement she was about to enter. Not even Mother Nature approved of this match, Evelina thought to herself as she walked to where *he* was waiting.

An angry numbness weighed down her insides. She'd often imagined this day but had always believed she would marry for love. Now she was marrying simply to ensure she had a home, prospects of her own, and she did not bring more scandal to her family.

*Plus, you do find Lord Raine attractive.*

*Stop that!*

He was a rake and could never be faithful, she reminded herself. *Oh no!* A dreadful thought entered her mind. What if Lord Raine disregarded her terms and expected a wedding night? Evelina had assumed she'd made her point when she told him that neither of them would get what they wanted, but did he understand that meant she was not prepared to consummate the marriage as well?

"Thank you for coming," Lord Raine said in a tone which suggested he believed Evelina might have cried off. Little did he realize just how close she'd come to running away, but in every scenario she'd devised, her prospects were worse than enduring this farce of a marriage.

"As if she had much of a choice." Her brother's angry words, hushed as they were, pierced the clear morning air as he approached their party, his wife following close behind.

*Now* Harold showed up. *Now* Harold was playing the protective older brother. Where was he when Mama took ill, and then Father? Why hadn't he called out Lord Raine? Harold had never even asked *her* what had happened at Lady Holland's ball.

"Darling, please behave yourself," Rachel, or rather Lady Grace as she preferred to be addressed, said as she brushed past Evelina, leaving a trail of jasmine drifting behind her. Oh, how Evelina detested that scent. It was forever ruined by her sister-in-law.

Evelina didn't know what her sister-in-law hoped to gain, but she was clearly enjoying herself which was, by its very nature, somewhat worrying. Hopefully, after today, Evelina would not have to see Rachel for a very long time. That was at least one positive outcome of marrying. Now if she could only find a dozen more, perhaps she could survive the loveless union.

"Rachel," Aunt Imogene started in a firm tone, ignoring the title Rachel preferred, "Join me in the church."

Rachel was clearly a little frightened by Aunt Imogene, for without even the slightest hesitation she did as she was told and followed the older woman.

Lord Raine stepped closer to Evelina, in a most possessive manner, which she did not care for. "Before we begin, may I have a moment alone with my bride?"

Harold eyed Evelina, then spoke to Lord Raine. "You may talk to her over by that tree, while I stand right here watching to ensure nothing untoward happens."

*Untoward?* Evelina had already been kissed by Lord Raine in front of dozens of guests at Lady Holland's ball and compelled to accept his hand. What did Harold think would happen outside the church?

It was as if her thoughts traveled from her mind to her sister's lips, only in a tamer tone. "Oh really, Harold, be serious. He just wants to talk," Alexandra scolded.

Lord Raine began to move toward the indicated tree and seemed to expect Evelina to follow. She would indulge him today, but she would not be at his beck and call. When she glanced to her sisters for aid, they each gave her a supportive look, encouraging her to go to where *he* awaited. Evelina assumed they took her quietness today as nervousness for what was to come *tonight*. Before they'd left the house, both Alexandra and Theodora advised her to just relax and enjoy her wedding night. Little did they know, there would be no wedding night.

"You wanted to speak with me?" she asked as she came near him, not even trying to hide her annoyance.

"We need to discuss the terms of this marriage," he began in a serious tone as if this were some sort of business contract that she had a say in. "As I've said, I require an heir and—"

She interrupted with a stern voice. "I require love." She shook her head, and took in a deep breath, hoping to ease her fraying nerves. This was not the time or place to be having this discussion. How could she make him understand that she wanted a family with love, not a union with the sole purpose of simply providing an heir? What words were there that would even begin to sway his opinion at that moment? She took in a deep breath. Best to just get the day over with. "There's nothing more to discuss now." And with those words, she walked back to where her sisters were standing. She took them arm in arm, then started toward the church.

"What was all that about?" Theodora whispered.

"Nothing, just a little disagreement about some nonsensical topic that can be discussed later."

"Evelina?" Her eldest sister drew out her name in inquiry.

She looked into her sister's concerned eyes. She could not worry either of them with her woes. Evelina pasted on a smile and, in what she hoped was a convincing voice, said, "It is truly nothing, I assure you."

Alexandra and Theodora glanced at each other, but neither said a word. Whether they believed her or not was beside the point. The annoyance and anger she felt a moment ago was replaced with humiliation. She would not discuss her worries with them. She would not discuss them with anyone.

EVELINA HAD WALKED away from him. From him! No woman had ever walked away from him. Quite the contrary. Women tended to search him out, follow him, make demands. And here was the one woman, the one that was to be his wife, who not only did not fawn over him, but could barely stand to be next to him for any length of time. *And* she was driving him mad with want.

Lord Grace eyed him, then nodded his head toward the church, indicating it was time. James should be nervous or anxious or . . . or some other ominous feeling, but for reasons he could not comprehend, regardless of Evelina's current disdain for him, he felt at ease with the situation.

The ceremony was short and to the point. If not for the brimming smiles of Evelina's sisters and great-aunt, one would have thought that someone had just been sentenced to death rather than joined in holy matrimony.

A short time later, he was ensconced in his carriage with his new bride, returning to his mother's home for the wedding breakfast. Although she was quite vocal over her displeasure with the match—which was a mild way to put it—she'd informed James that she was prepared to put on a good show for the *ton* since she remained unable to host a proper wedding with a proper groom for Daisy. At the very least, Daisy did not have to witness their mother's antics, and was instead enjoying newly married life in the country. James hoped to be doing the same very soon.

As the carriage rolled along, an awkward, uncomfortable silence filled the space, creating tension that he wanted to eradicate.

*Say something.*

Numerous thoughts and words collided in his mind before he settled on one. "Perhaps I should not have stated so ineloquently what I expected from this marriage." She didn't say a word but waited for him to elaborate. She held his gaze, a deep penetrating gaze that did foreign things to his insides. His words were always carefully decided upon before he spoke, but she didn't know that about him. He needed to use this skill to try to smooth things over with her. "This marriage can be enjoyable for both of us even without love," he said in a seductive tone meant to tempt her.

Her retort was quick and without any sympathetic emotion. "I am not interested in having a baby with someone I do not love."

"It is your duty!" He ran a frustrated hand through his hair, his determination to choose his words carefully shattering to dust. "Any wife would be more than happy to enjoy the pleasures of the bed without—"

"Not any wife. Not all wives. Perhaps you should have considered that *before* you kissed *me*," she replied in a smug tone.

What was it about this woman that caused him to lose all sense of reason and control?

"I didn't *want* to *want* to kiss you."

Something electric passed between them as she just stared at him, almost in disbelief. Her eyes narrowed slightly, as if trying to read his thoughts. Those deep green eyes that reminded him of springtime emerging after a cold, dark winter.

*Dammit.* He hadn't meant for her to know how much he desired her. Once a woman knew a man desired her, she soon took full advantage, demanding her wants and needs, dangling—

*This isn't about the other women you've bedded. This is Evelina. She's different,* his heart begged him to recall, but his mind remembered every tactic used for betrayal.

The electricity surging between them grew. The quick rise and fall of her chest and her desire-filled eyes indicated she was just as affected as he was. He wanted to pull her onto his lap and show her the desire surging through his veins.

And then the carriage came to a stop.

She blinked several times, as if trying to break the spell, then slid closer toward the door.

James did not want his bride to be afraid of him or of the mutual desire clearly simmering between them. He would bide his time. "I have never forced a woman, and I do not intend to start now. I will not come to your bed uninvited."

"Does that mean you will seek pleasure elsewhere?" Her words were full of accusation, as if he'd already committed the crime and she was sentencing him to castration.

Evelina's question took him aback. She didn't want his attentions, and yet it seemed as if she was demanding fidelity. Whatever her thoughts on the subject, he had no interest in any other women, and without a doubt he would not become his father. He had made that promise to himself years ago.

"No. I have no intention of dishonoring our vows." And with that declaration, he exited the conveyance and prepared to put on a good show for their guests.

As the morning dragged on and on, much to James' surprise, Evelina did not display any of the malcontent she had in the carriage. Quite the opposite in fact. He suspected that being a good hostess had been drilled into her over the years. She was the epitome of a beautiful bride except for one minor yet important fact: she did not want to be married to him.

James would simply have to change her mind.

# Chapter Five

SINCE THEIR WEDDING nearly a month ago, James had tried everything he could think of to get to know Evelina better. He'd presented her with large bouquets of flowers filled with lilies, lilacs, jasmine, violets, roses, and even chrysanthemums, but she reproached him for being insincere because he clearly did not know her favorite. He'd tried to tempt her with culinary delicacies, but she simply scrunched her nose and turned away. And then there was the ultimate disaster . . . a new gown! Evelina had informed him that she was not his mistress and would not dress like one.

He'd hoped that removing to the country, away from the gossiping *ton*, would have aided his cause as well, but nothing he'd done had softened her resolve toward him. He was at his wits' end. He meant what he'd said—he would never force himself on her, but he'd never been in such a predicament where the woman he wanted didn't want him.

To make matters worse, Evelina and his mother were constantly arguing. The only thing his mother and wife agreed upon was their mutual disdain for one another. With each passing day, he felt as if his world was spiraling more and more out of control and all he could do was watch.

They could not go on like this forever. One way or another

this would end today.

THE FORMIDABLE LADY Raine walked into the breakfast room plainly prepared to do battle . . . again. Her narrow gaze surveyed Evelina, almost as if determining how she would torment her today. Every day was something new and horrible with this woman. Everything from subtle slights meant to undermine Evelina's confidence to brazen comments about Evelina's unsuitability as a viscountess and lack of decorum. Evelina knew her worth and would not let this woman affect that knowledge, but it was still tiring just the same and made her miss her own dearest mama all the more.

It was just Evelina's luck to end up with a mother-in-law such as her. It was bad enough that she had found herself in a loveless marriage, but now she also had to endure the unpleasantness this woman spewed in her direction every time they were near each other. Which seemed to be quite frequently. Evelina could not shake the feeling that the older woman thought she would run off with the silver in the middle of the night.

"Good morning, Lady Raine," Evelina greeted in her best attempt at a pleasant tone. Although she was not happy about her current living arrangements, she tried to seize what joy she could, and since Evelina's amiable countenance appeared to annoy Lady Raine, she did it all the more.

"There is nothing good about this morning, or the previous thirty since my son was *forced* to marry you and—"

*There was a limit as to how amiable one could be in the presence of Lady Raine*, Evelina thought as she started to argue, "I assure you I had nothing to do—"

"You kissed him!" Lady Raine's voice ricocheted through the room, rattling the cups and saucers.

In the calmest voice Evelina could muster, she firmly stated, "*He* kissed me." The moment those three words left her mouth, she knew Lady Raine was not pleased. Her cheeks deepened to a fiery red as she pursed her lips, contemplating her next words.

If the numerous remarks her new sister-in-law, Daisy, had made at meetings of the Three Graces Salon last Season were any indication, Evelina suspected Lady Raine did not have any fondness for her children. However, she also suspected that the woman would defend her family's honor until her last breath, regardless of what might be true or what harm may come to others. Evelina had never trusted Lady Raine, now less than ever.

"That is beside the point! And I know exactly what went on at that . . . that so-called salon you and your sisters hosted. You've ruined many lives!" Lady Raine bellowed.

Before Evelina had a chance to defend herself further, Lord Raine burst into the room, eyeing them both. She sucked in a deep breath and braced herself for a weak diversion or for him to take his mother's side. His attempts so far at smoothing things over between Evelina and his mother had always had a less than desirable outcome, usually resulting in him just leaving the room in frustration. Evelina was convinced that Lady Raine did not wish to keep any sort of peace.

Then, much to her surprise, he turned a hard gaze, not on her, but his own mother. "That's enough! You insisted on staying in the country with us, but you have made life miserable for Evelina and everyone else this past month."

*Probably longer*, Evelina thought to herself. She could not imagine Lady Raine ever having been pleasant to be around. And then it dawned on her. Not only had Lord Raine issued a firm reprimand to his mother, but he'd defended her as well. Was he hoping to gain her favor with such actions? But why would he risk his mother's wrath in the process?

Evelina was trying to puzzle out the question when she noticed Lady Raine about to argue. However, before she could utter so much as a syllable, Lord Raine stated, "I think you'll be much happier in London, Mother. You'll depart at first light tomorrow morning."

Although his tone brooked no argument, Lady Raine would

clearly not let her son have the final say. She squared her shoulders, then began in a haughty tone, "I believe I shall depart for London tomorrow, as I am obviously unappreciated here." As she turned to take her leave, she shot Evelina a harsh warning glance that sent a chill down her spine, rattling her senses.

Lord Raine moved to where Evelina was standing, and without thought, she took several steps away from him, moving closer to the wall. He let out an exasperated sigh, but Evelina couldn't tell if it was meant for her or his mother.

"I apologize for my mother's behavior."

"You have nothing to apologize for. It's her behavior." Although Evelina was not content with her current situation, Lord Raine could not be blamed for his mother's actions.

"I apologize just the same."

"Thank you," she offered. He had stood up for her, and for that, she appreciated his efforts.

"We should have parted ways following the wedding breakfast." The lines edging his deep brown eyes softened as he changed the subject. "Since we're in this for life, do you not agree it would be beneficial if we get to know one another?"

"I suppose." She truly could not fathom what they may have in common, but she supposed being on cordial terms with the man she had married was better than constant conflict and disdain. Though she was certain she already knew all there was to know about him—he was a rake, pure and simple—perhaps if they *did* find some common ground, she could live a more peaceful life, here in the country. "I'll begin. I like long walks."

"I prefer to ride my horse."

"I enjoy reading, especially poetry and—" The scrunch of his nose told her he did not enjoy poetry. "Dancing?"

"I find it barely tolerable." His confession was a sting to her heart.

*No poetry. No dancing.* This was hopeless.

"Lord Raine—"

"James," he corrected her in a deep tone that stirred something deep within.

But she was not ready to be on such intimate terms. She was still coming to terms with everything that had happened and held firm in her desire for love. She eyed him, then emphasized the only name she was willing to refer to him by at this time. "Lord Raine, it is clear we have nothing in common."

"I highly doubt we have *nothing* in common," the words dripped with another meaning.

What was he trying to do?

*Use his rakish ways against you.* Well, Evelina would have none of that.

As a girl, she'd tried to imagine what her future husband would look like. He would be tall and handsome. *Just like Lord Raine.* With a deep voice that excited her soul. *Just like Lord Raine.*

*Stop that!*

Evelina was not so unreasonable as to be unable to admit that Lord Raine cut a fine figure. But even before their wedding, and especially since their arrival in the country, she'd been avoiding him and the desire he stirred. A marriage may require some level of attraction for one's partner, but attraction alone didn't make for a long happy life together. And although the feelings he stirred were quite intoxicating, they were far too burdensome. She may find him physically appealing, but that was where it ended. Lord Raine did not possess the most important qualities: a caring heart, an understanding soul, the desire to be a good person, and a love for poetry.

She cleared her throat and attempted to pick up the thread of their conversation again. "You are clearly not close with your family, but I am with my sisters and aunt. Family is most important."

"I agree with you on that."

He agreed? What was he up to?

"I prefer the country, and given your reputation, you obviously prefer Town." She hadn't meant to sound so smug, but she was trying to make a point of their unsuitability.

"You think you know me, my type, so well." His gaze penetrated into the depths of her soul, stirring all sorts of tingles. "I may have to prove you wrong."

"I think it is you who will be proven wrong, Lord Raine." He started toward her, and her pulse increased, her thoughts becoming cloudy. No. She would not allow him to affect her so. She squared her shoulders, held her chin high, and presented her case. "You do not enjoy poetry or activities that I like—such as dancing and taking walks. Rather, these are things that you detest. I could list a dozen more reasons why we don't suit, why—"

He closed the distance between them but did not touch her. He was close, so close. *Too close.* Heat radiated between them, encircling them. He stared down into her upturned face, and she fought to control the rising desire that tempted her to reach up and caress his smooth cheek, or . . . *kiss his delectable lips.*

*No.* Hold your ground, she demanded of herself.

Seconds passed and still he did not say a word. They were at a deadlock, each too proud to relent.

And then, in the blink of an eye, Lord Raine took two steps back, never breaking her gaze.

"Damn you, Evelina!" And with that he stormed from the room, leaving her more confused than she'd ever been in her entire life.

JAMES HAD ALMOST kissed his wife, almost claimed what was rightfully his. He'd made a promise and he would not break it. But he could not stay and endure the torture of being near his wife and not being able to touch her, kiss her.

There was only one thing he could do. Leave. Evelina would remain in the country, and he would go to his estate near London. She soon would become a distant memory and he would stop desiring her.

There was only one problem. He did not think he would ever stop desiring his wife.

# Chapter Six

*Six months later*

E VELINA WAS PERFECTLY content with the absence of Lord
Raine *and* his mother. After their last argument six months
ago, James left a letter informing Evelina of his decision to leave
her in the country. Being sequestered in the country at Raine Hall
suited her just fine, and before long, all the angst and worries that
she'd been experiencing over the past year had dissipated, and all
that remained were pleasant days spent relishing her new role.

As much as she disliked her mother-in-law, she could not
fault the woman on her ability to maintain such a beautiful house
and property. Prior to Lady Raine leaving, she'd expressed her
displeasure at having to relinquish her role as mistress of Raine
Hall to the care of Evelina. The older woman had grumbled that
her beloved home was certain to fall to ruin under Evelina's
undiscerning eye.

With each passing day, she rose further above Lady Raine's
insults. For the first time in Evelina's life, she felt as if she had true
purpose. Granted, creating the salon with her sisters had been
meaningful, but this was different. She was managing the estate
all on her own. Evelina found great peace in learning her new
role as viscountess and was never without something to do.

Even Alexandra and Theodora had come to visit for a brief
week, making her contentment nearly complete, though she still

had not revealed what had had happened between her and Lord Raine and made excuses for his absence, citing estate business. She suspected they hadn't believed her, though, and counseled Evelina that if she just gave it time, things would get better between herself and Lord Raine. She supposed the first step would be to think of him as her true husband instead of Lord Raine, but she wasn't quite ready for that. Thinking of him as her husband suggested certain intimacies, intimacies that could result in a child. No, she held firm to her belief that a baby should be born out of love. So she took her sisters' advice with gentle good humor, then went about her business.

As days turned into months, she found more and more joy in tending to the many duties dictated by her new station. Her favorite by far was making baskets full of foodstuffs and visiting the tenants. Evelina was determined to know every tenant. She wanted to know their characters, their troubles and difficulties. She wanted to help. Over the past months, she felt she *had* helped and had gained a better understanding of not only the people, but also the land.

But Evelina knew the quiet solitude wouldn't last. One day, she would have to see Lord Raine again. And then what?

She wouldn't think about that today.

The rain had stopped, and the clouds had parted, revealing a clear blue sky. Evelina enjoyed days such as this with the sunlight streaming into the parlor after days on end of gloom. It gave her soul hope for the future.

One more task to complete, then she would take full advantage of this glorious day. She had many ideas for tenant improvements, but those would require Lord Raine's approval. She'd been composing her thoughts on paper, wanting to make certain that her requests were reasonable and would not be refused when she wrote him. She was rereading her requests one final time when Fendall entered.

"Pardon me, Lady Raine," the butler began, "Lord Raine has just arrived and has requested your presence in his study."

*Lord Raine was here?* Her heart pounded against her chest, whether from nervousness or excitement she could not tell. Whether nervousness or excitement, it quickly gave way to a different emotion altogether. Annoyance. Why did he have to break her solitude without so much as a warning? Granted, it was his house, too, but it would have been polite to give her some notice. Evelina liked to be prepared, or at the very least, feel prepared.

Within the span of a few minutes, her calm world had been turned upside down once again by Lord Raine. Why couldn't he just let her be? She thought to argue, but the peace she'd found over the past months begged her to maintain it, to nurture it.

She swallowed hard, then said, "Thank you, Fendall." She glanced down at her notes. It was probably best that she wait to see what Lord Raine wanted before presenting him with her list, or arguing with him for that matter. With a little reluctance, she stood and went to his study.

FOR THE PAST six months, James had kept his distance, not only from Evelina, but from the rest of his family as well. He'd become a veritable hermit, trapped in his own unfulfilled longings. His siblings assumed he was enjoying marital bliss. How far from correct they were. He'd been staying at his estate a quarter day's journey from London. From there, he'd been able to tend to business but, more importantly, avoid seeing his mother, despite her constant demands for him to visit so he could deal with whatever issue she was currently having.

Although he'd separated himself from everyone, Evelina was never far from his thoughts. During his isolation, he had plenty of time to contemplate their future, but he had not even come close to figuring out what to do. And then one dreary day, the answer came in a letter.

His cousin, Jessica, was to make her debut this Season but Aunt Silvia had taken ill and was unable to fulfill chaperoning duties for her daughter. Uncle Aaron was most sincere in his request, inquiring whether James and his wife would chaperone the young lady. While James had never been close to either of his parents, Uncle Aaron had always embraced James and his youngest sister, Daisy, enveloping them within the folds of his own immediate family. Time spent with his father's youngest brother had been some of the happiest of his youth.

James would do anything for his uncle and his family. Plus, chaperoning his cousin was the perfect excuse to see his wife again. With time, he hoped to develop a more solid plan, but at the very least, he had a reason to see her once again.

A week later he arrived at Raine Hall. As he strolled into the house he'd known his whole life, it didn't take long to notice that something was different. It seemed almost brighter, happier, uniquely Evelina. He shook those thoughts away. Surely a house made of masonry and wood could not exhibit emotion. He must be more tired and anxious to see his wife than he had first realized.

Upon his arrival, he went straight to his study and sent word to his wife. He'd dreamed about her more than he was willing to admit over the past months. Would her lips be as lush, ready for kissing, as they had been before? Would she be happy to see him? Or would her eyes still hold anger and disdain?

"I see you've returned," Evelina said as she entered the study, the tone of her words filled with caution and uncertainty. At least they didn't hold the same contempt he'd remembered from the last time they'd spoken.

Although her eyes were cold, she looked absolutely beautiful in a blush-colored morning dress that accentuated her curves and brought out a delectable rosy hue on her skin. Yes, her lips were as lush as he remembered.

Dammit, but how was he to win her favor? Or at the very least, soften her resolve. Desperation weighed his insides down.

James was desperate to know his wife, not only physically, but simply her—herself.

One of his father's many lectures echoed in the dark recesses of his mind. *A woman can destroy you, destroy what truly matters. Remember that, boy. You will be a viscount one day. All that matters in this world is money, status, and breeding. Seek pleasure, but always remember your duty to the title.*

After six long months apart from the woman who'd constantly haunted every moment of his life, James knew his late sire's words were false. But the question remained: what truly mattered? Pleasure was . . . well, pleasurable, but he was craving so much more.

"Good afternoon, Evelina. I come in peace," he said with a smile he hoped conveyed the sincerity he felt.

She let out a long sigh, but didn't argue or tell him not to use her given name. It was a small victory, and one he would gladly take.

"Please have a seat." She took the seat across from him, keeping her posture rigid. He didn't want her to be nervous or anxious around him, but he didn't know what to say without blundering. *Best to stick to the reason why you're here.* "I am in need of your assistance," he said.

She raised a delicate auburn brow. "Oh?"

"My cousin, Jessica, is in need of a chaperone for the Season and—"

"There is much to be done here. Why can't you mother take on that role?"

James let out a long sigh. "My mother does not care for anyone on my father's side of the family and with Daisy now enceinte, the responsibility has fallen to us." He paused, framing his words carefully. "I had hoped to entice you back to London for the Season. I have full faith in your chaperoning skills and would be grateful to leave the specifics of Jessica's Season up to you."

THE MOMENT EVELINA had walked into the study, she knew she was in trouble. Although he was seated behind the desk, she couldn't help but notice the fine figure he cut or take her eyes off Lord Raine. He was more handsome than she remembered. Worse, she could not control the surge of want and need, annoyance and anger, that she felt. She fought to control her emotions, to stay calm and neutral, but something in his countenance called to her. And then he asked her to chaperone Jessica.

Evelina was very fond of Jessica, having spent several days with the young lady as she was journeying through these parts to return home from school last month. But it meant another Season in London.

It was one thing to be married, living alone in the country, and quite another to be married, sharing a residence in London with her husband, during the Season where they would have to attend functions together, where all eyes would be on them, assessing their marriage. Still, she might be able to hold the Three Graces Salon again, where she could aid other ladies as they gathered *on dits* about the *ton*, while delving into forbidden topics, so they may not fall victim to the same trap she had.

The least she could do was to hear him out. "What would be expected of me?"

James' eyes bore into her. She could almost feel the hunger and desire in those luscious brown eyes. *Oh dear*, perhaps this wasn't a good idea after all.

He did not break eye contact as he clenched his jaw, seemingly fighting the same thoughts she was. A moment later, he cleared his throat, business as usual. "Chaperoning at events—which would fall largely on you—hosting a ball, several dinner parties . . . the usual sorts of events." Evelina was about to ask the one question that would definitely sway her answer, when he stated, "And my mother will be remaining at her own residence."

That *was* a relief. "And *if* I agree?"

He stood, rounded the desk, then stopped in front of her, looking more roguish than ever. His eyes skimmed her face, then down farther, settling on her rising chest. Could he hear the pounding of her heart growing louder with each breath she took?

"What do you want, Evelina?" The deep, suggestive words sent a shiver of anticipation up her neck.

"I want . . ." Her mouth suddenly felt dry, and she couldn't control her breathing.

His eyes deepened with desire as he waited for her to finish her sentence.

*Focus. Do not give into a rake, it will only lead to heartache.*

What she truly wanted she could not have, but she *would not* succumb to the charms of a rake, even if he was her husband.

She forced the rising desire down into the depths of her being, then raised her chin. Now was the opportunity to secure her future. "To return to the country and continue to oversee the running of Raine Hall and its tenants as soon as the Season is over. I have many ideas and would like the freedom to implement them."

His features remained unchanged. There was no hesitation when he responded with a single word that held an almost enticing innuendo, "Agreed."

Confusion and bewilderment laced her thoughts. He had not asked any questions about what sort of improvements she wanted to make, how much they would cost, or anything of that nature. What game was Lord Raine playing?

Evelina suspected she'd just made a deal with the devil himself.

## Chapter Seven

T HE SEVERAL DAYS' journey to London passed in slow, agonizing measures. James had not wanted to say the wrong thing, and so kept quiet during the journey. Even when they'd stopped at coaching inns along the way, he'd kept a respectful distance, ensuring her comfort—and his agony—in separate rooms.

Even now as he watched her, nose in a book, he didn't know if his wife was truly content reading, or if it was just a ruse to torture him. If he were less of a gentleman, he would have found a better way to occupy their time, namely seducing his wife.

Today they would arrive in town and hopefully he would be able to create some distance and regain his senses. He shifted once again in the seat, trying not to think of the single kiss he'd shared with her, and the way her mouth had succumbed to his ministrations, how the warmth from her body fired his soul, and—

*Stop this madness! Stop thinking about her.*

By the time they reached London, James' head was pounding, and he was in desperate need of a strong drink and quiet solitude, but that would have to wait.

"Good evening, Lord Raine," his butler said. "Everything has been made ready and a light dinner will be served as soon as you're ready."

"Thank you, Norman. Efficient as always." He looked past the butler to Evelina. She looked as worn out as he felt. Had the closeness of the journey affected her as much as it had him, or was she just tired from travel? "I believe we will eat first."

Before long, James and his wife were ensconced in the smaller of the two dining rooms. He used this room last Season when his youngest sister was in residence, enjoying quiet meals away from their mother, who always had a knack of souring one's stomach.

Despite the intimate setting, there was still too much distance in his estimation, but at the very least, Evelina was talking with him.

"Tell me more about your cousin," she requested. "When Jessica visited for those few days, she chattered on about school and how much she missed Daisy, but not much else."

His laughter filled the room. "Those two are so similar. When they were younger, they often mimicked each other, much to my mother's dismay."

Evelina's laughter mingled with his. Hers was a pleasant, solid laugh, not superficial or forced. "I can imagine the mischief those two got into."

"Much like you and your sisters?" he teased.

"Not at all," she said with a half-smile, making him suspect that she and her sisters had stirred up quite a lot of mischief indeed. "And what of her family?"

James was enjoying the evening with Evelina. It was a pleasant change from the tense journey here. He didn't want Evelina to be on edge or annoyed with him. This was a good start to the Season.

"Uncle Aaron is the youngest of my father's siblings. Jessica is their only child and they dote on her, but she is not spoiled or insincere. My aunt and uncle have high hopes for a good match." The moment the words left his mouth, he regretted them. A good match and a love match were two different things, and without a doubt, he knew his wife's opinion as to which was preferable.

Evelina gave him a sideways glance, but thankfully chose not to pursue that point. Or rather, chose not to pursue it at that moment, and continued with her questions. "Has she been well prepared for the Season?"

"Yes. Aunt Silvia made certain Jessica was well educated, and well-versed in all the diversions becoming of a young woman of the *ton*. Plus, she has a dowry of three thousand."

"Not a paltry sum," Evelina said, then raised her fork to her mouth. Her lips parted as she took a bite of the meat pie.

How in bloody hell did the woman make eating meat pie look seductive? James swallowed hard as he shifted in his seat. The remainder of the meal passed with pleasant conversation about the Season, but always on the edge of James' thoughts was Evelina herself, and how enticing she looked this evening in a light blue satin evening dress.

The moment the meal was over, he decided he could not wait any longer for a stiff drink. He was about to excuse himself and retreat to his study when Evelina caught him completely off guard.

"Do you mind if I join you for brandy?"

"I wasn't aware that you enjoyed liquor." He went to the side cabinet and grabbed two glasses and the decanter.

There was so much about his wife that he didn't know. He wanted to know her likes and dislikes—besides himself, of course—her favorite color and flower, what occupied her thoughts. He just wanted to know her. He hoped with time, he would discover those answers.

Those ponderings took him aback for a moment. Never in his life had he wanted to know more about a woman's interests. He felt as if he was treading on dangerous ground.

She let out a mischievous laugh, which he found far too enticing. "Oh yes. When my sisters and I hosted our salon, we decided that the ladies should experience brandy *and* cigars. Just to see what all the fuss was about." There were so many—too many—

questions swirling through his thoughts, but before he could ask even one, Evelina added with gentle humor, "Oh, don't worry, your sister partook as well."

That was not one of the questions that even had crossed his mind. "Why am I not surprised?" he said with a shake of his head as he handed Evelina a glass.

Evelina brought the glass of amber liquid to her mouth. She inhaled as if relishing in the strong scent, then slowly, seductively touched it to her lips and tilted it slightly as the amber liquid traveled toward her lips. She took in a sip, closed her eyes, and swallowed. It was the most inappropriate, yet enticing, act he'd ever witness a lady do. He wanted those lips on him.

*Lord give him strength.*

James did not know how much longer he could endure such torture without pulling his wife into his embrace and showing her just how much she affected him. Without further thought he stood, made some inane excuse and left the room. It was going to be a long Season in residence with his delectable wife.

LORD RAINE AND Evelina had only been in London two days and the gossip had already started. Rumors were circulating of their scandalous kiss, followed by a hasty marriage and subsequent departure to the country, not to mention their separate living conditions.

Evelina had thought after so many months, more-tantalizing gossip would have caught the attention of the rumormongers. How was she to aid Jessica, who was due to arrive tomorrow, in finding a suitable match if her own name was constantly on the gossips' tongues? What proper gentleman would want to embroil himself in such a family? And she hadn't even held one salon. She could only imagine what would be said if the Three Graces Salon resurfaced. Evelina would just have to take extra precautions when she did host one.

If her sisters were in Town, she would be able to discuss the current situation with them and formulate a plan on how to combat the gossipmongers, but she didn't want to bother either of them with a letter full of her woes. Alexandra was enjoying preparing for motherhood and Theodora had her hands full with a houseful of puppies. Even Aunt Imogene had yet to return to Town, having extended her time visiting with friends in Bath. There was no reason at all for her family to be present. They each had their own lives and their own responsibilities now. Such was the way of the world.

Evelina felt utterly alone. She didn't know who to turn to for advice. She let out a long sigh. There was really only one person left to turn to.

Her husband.

With some reluctance she walked through the house toward his study. She'd never searched him out before and didn't know what to expect. Would he be annoyed by her presence? Would he be as angry as she was with all the gossip? Would he even know what to do?

He'd certainly been embroiled in enough scandals through the years that he should be able to offer some words of advice. But then again, she suspected his way of dealing with gossip was just to stir more.

By the time she faced the closed study door, she wondered if this was truly a good idea. She was about to turn around when common sense reared its annoying head. She couldn't go at this alone.

*You have no choice.*

Bringing her hand up, she knocked firmly on the rich mahogany door and waited.

"Come in." His deep voice was not quite short, but not friendly just the same, which only added to the anxiety she'd been feeling since reading the gossip sheet.

She said a silent prayer as she opened the door, then entered the space, closing the door behind her. "I need some advice."

The moment she spoke, he raised his gaze from the ledger he'd been reading. As their eyes met, her heart started pounding. Why did this always happen when he looked at her?

"What sort of advice?" His tone gave nothing away, and she could not discern whether he was happy at her request or not.

She went straight to the issue at hand. "What are we going to do about the gossip?"

"I'm not aware of any—"

Worry had worn her patience thin this morning, and she cut him off rather abruptly. "You have not heard the rumors circulating about our marriage?"

The morning sun streaming into the study window highlighted his lovely blond hair and handsome features. He stood and rounded the desk. As he moved toward her, her knees started to wobble.

"Why do you care?"

She swallowed hard as those deep brown eyes assessed her. She fought through the flutters multiplying in her stomach. *Focus on why you're here.* "How am I to aid your cousin if gossip is constantly laid at our doorstep?"

"It will pass," he offered with nonchalance as if it were every day that a woman was pushed into marrying a rake. Did he not understand the severity of the situation?

"It's been more than six months and it hasn't dissipated one bit, and now the Season is about to begin and—"

"Do you truly care what the gossips say, what they think?" His question was bold and direct, much like his gaze on her.

Heat rushed to her cheeks. "No. Do you?"

She was only concerned for how this might affect his cousin. Truly she did not. *Yes, you do. No,* she argued with herself. *I only care how this will affect Jessica.*

A deep sigh coursed through her. She *did* care, and therein lay part of the problem. In the past, when gossip circulated about the Three Graces Salon, it hadn't affected her as much because she knew that she and her sisters were doing something good in aiding young ladies, and they faced it together. In the end, that was idle gossip, but the rumors currently circulating about their marriage were a vicious attack that shook her to her core, all the more because she'd been trying to avoid even the hint of further scandal. Since arriving in Town, she had not misstepped once.

Evelina was... well, there were no words for the turmoil swirling in her. And all Lord Raine could do was sit there, which only added to her frustration over the situation. Damn, if it weren't for him, her name would not be sullied in the first place.

"Aren't you going to answer my question?" she pressed. "This doesn't only affect Jessica, but me and . . . us, too. Aren't you the least bit concerned?" As the question exited her mouth, she realized that she wasn't *just* asking about the gossip at hand.

He ran a hand through his hair, disrupting the perfect coiffure. Somehow, he looked even more handsome with tousled hair. "What do you want me to say Evelina?" His question seemed to hold a different meaning.

Suddenly, her original intent for coming in faded, replaced by the one thought that had continued to plague her all these months. "I want to know why you kissed me that night on the veranda, in front of everyone, forcing us both into this inconvenient marriage."

And suddenly he was storming across the room, backing her against the closed door, his arms braced on either side of her. But she wasn't frightened of him. Quite the contrary.

His words came low and hot, and were far too intoxicating to her. "Because ever since that night we first met, I have thought of nothing else but kissing you. Do you not understand that at every turn you seduce me?"

He had *wanted* to kiss her?

With each breath she took, her heart sped up, matching the rise and fall of her chest. How was that possible? He could have any woman he wanted, and even if only a fraction of the rumors were true, he'd had quite the sampling of actresses, opera singers, and voluptuous courtesans. She had no experience, no pleasure to offer.

His words were low, gravelly. "It would be best if you took your leave."

She was about to argue when he stepped away. His features were flushed and his temper seemed barely contained.

This man was so odious! One moment he was brushing off gossip, the next, telling her that she was constantly seducing him, and then in the next breath dismissing her. He wasn't listening to her. He wasn't talking to her.

If that was how he wanted to play the game, so be it. Evelina held her head high, and without another word, left the room.

# Chapter Eight

O NCE JESSICA ARRIVED, it was a whirlwind of activity getting ready for the Season. Her mother had indeed prepared her daughter well, but there were still last-minute fittings and miscellaneous items to purchase. The activities and social obligations were only just beginning, but all the bustle provided a much-needed reprieve from all the other things that had been consuming her thoughts.

The first couple of events had come and gone with great success, and the invitations continued to fill the silver salver. The Season was off to a good start, for Jessica at least. Though she was pleased it didn't seem to be doing Jessica any harm so far, the gossip surrounding Evelina and James had unfortunately not abated even in the slightest, and Evelina constantly found herself in the predicament of having to avoid questions about her husband and ignore stares.

She suspected tonight would be much the same.

"Remember that Lady Pynes is most particular that a young lady be demure, respectful, and only speak when spoken to," Evelina reminded her young charge. "And when introduced to Lady Martel, whatever you do, do not stare at the rather large blemish on her chin. She is not to be crossed."

"Do's and don'ts," Jessica said with a deep sigh. "There are too many. How will I ever remember them all?"

"It will get easier with time and experience," Evelina soothed.

If only she believed her own words. It certainly had not gotten easier with time where Lord Raine was concerned. And if experience had taught her anything, it was that the *ton* was predictably unpredictable, forever stirring headaches and woes.

*Just like your husband.*

They seemed to constantly be at odds these days, ever since that moment in his study, and yet she could not stop thinking about him. And every time she heard his deep, masculine voice, a ripple of desire shot through her body. But she didn't want a marriage based solely on desire.

The carriage came to a halt, disrupting her thoughts. Soon, they were waiting to be introduced with dozens of other guests. It seemed as if the entire *ton*, in all its opulence, was present this evening. She shouldn't have been surprised. Lady Pynes' grand ball was considered one of the premier events to start the Season. A young lady's performance here set the stage for the remainder of the Season.

As they approached their hostess, Evelina sucked in her breath and said a silent prayer that she would not be questioned about how she was enjoying married life or about her husband's whereabouts, as he had yet to make an appearance at a Society event this Season.

"Good evening, Lady Raine, Miss Raine." Their hostess glanced about Evelina's side. "I see that Lord Raine is not attending this evening," Lady Pynes said with a raised brow and far too much curiosity for Evelina's taste.

"My husband is engaged elsewhere." That had become Evelina's standard response since re-entering Society. What was she supposed to say? The truth? That she had no idea where her husband was or how he filled his day.

Lady Pynes gave a nod of her head as if she didn't believe Evelina. "Yes, of course, engaged elsewhere," she dragged out the words, hinting at another meaning. "Enjoy your evening." Then she continued on, greeting the next guests.

As they strolled away from Lady Pynes, Jessica questioned under her breath, "Where *is* James this evening?"

"Engaged elsewhere," Evelina reiterated, the sourness of the words settling into her gut. She didn't want to think about *him*. And she certainly did not want to think about exactly where he'd run off to tonight, or any of the previous nights.

*Why do you care?*

*I don't.*

*Liar.*

The argument with herself was wearing thin.

What did she expect though? She wasn't his wife in the full sense of the word, and yet she expected fidelity.

*But you don't know that he hasn't been faithful,* she reminded herself, then shook her head. All these conflicting thoughts and emotions were tormenting her. She needed to reign in these emotions and focus on the present.

"Good evening, Lady Raine, Miss Raine," Mr. Drinkwater greeted. Before Evelina could return the salutation, he took in a deep breath and blurted, "May I have the next dance, Miss Raine?"

"I would be delighted." Jessica took his arm, and they strolled toward the dance floor.

A moment later, Miss Kitty Ashton rushed toward her. "Oh, Lady Raine! I was hoping to see you this evening."

"Good evening, Miss Ashton. How is your cousin doing?"

"Claudia is sailing the world with her Mr. Eastwick and couldn't be happier. I do hope she remembers to write often." She looked about, then lowered her voice. "I was hoping to attend one of your salons. My cousin said—"

"Kitty," the stern-faced Mrs. Ashton scowled as she approached. Claudia had warned the Grace sisters of her relations. It appeared she had not exaggerated in the least. "Mr. Simmons has been waiting his turn to dance with you all evening."

Kitty looked to Evelina and gave a slight roll of her eyes before turning back to her mother, defending her actions. "Mother, I was just inquiring after Lady Raine's sister, the Duchess of Blackburn."

Evelina suspected the name dropping was a ruse to soften Mrs. Ashton's displeasure. It was known throughout the *ton* that being in the good graces of a duchess could be a great asset in securing the best invitations.

The older woman looked to Evelina, then to her daughter. "I suppose that's acceptable." She then took a slight step away, as if to allow them some privacy to converse, but remained close enough to listen.

How was she to respond to Miss Ashton's request? With all the duties involved in chaperoning Jessica, Evelina had not had a moment to think about hosting the salon again, but perhaps she should consider it. Was she up for the challenge of hosting one without her sisters? She wasn't certain. Evelina could barely keep her own affairs in order.

So as to avoid Mrs. Ashton overhearing, Evelina kept her voice low, her response nondescript, neither confirming nor denying. "Perhaps in the near future the subject discussed may come to fruition."

A wide, enthusiastic smile encompassed Miss Kitty Ashton's features. "Oh, I hope so," she mouthed, then went to her mother's side, clearly pleased with the possibility of attending the salon.

Evelina watched as Jessica danced with Mr. Drinkwater. He was a pleasant fellow, albeit a little shy, but a rather clumsy dance partner. No sooner had the dance ended than Lord Lonsdale asked Jessica for the next set. Although a better dancer, he didn't appear as sincere in his attentions. Plus, he was a good friend of her husband, and rakes seemed to flock together.

Still, Jessica was quite the success that evening, and Evelina was certain that her ward would make a splendid match.

With her ward occupied for the remainder of the set, Evelina strolled toward the refreshment hall. She'd not taken even half a dozen steps, when she overheard the notorious gossipmonger, Lady Shephard, speaking in scandalized tones to a companion.

"A gentleman would have to be quite desperate to marry into *that* family. And did you hear," the woman lowered her voice, but the words were still loud and painfully clear to Evelina, "Lord Raine was seen in the arms of the Spanish opera singer, Señora de la Barca." Lady Shephard tsked several times then added, "I wouldn't expect him to be faithful to his wife. None of the Raine men ever were."

A heart-crushing pain struck her core. Could it be true? Had her husband been unfaithful already?

The room began to spin as thoughts of what she'd just heard overwhelmed her. Too consumed in her own dire musings, she hadn't realized the dance had ended or that Jessica had rejoined her until she spoke.

"Are you all right?" Jessica said with concern as she put a gentle hand on Evelina's forearm.

She couldn't let what she'd just overheard spoil Jessica's evening. She swallowed her pride and blinked away the tears, then opened her fan and with some drama, said, "It is rather warm this evening."

It was a tiresome excuse, overused by every member of the *ton*, but it was also the simplest one, and the one that consistently held true. Somehow, through a haze of hurt, she managed to make it through the evening, with none any more the wiser to her suffering.

By the time they'd returned to the house, all Evelina wanted to do was retire to her room and cry, but the moment she entered the foyer, it was clear that Fate had a different course in mind. Her husband was standing there, waiting. Waiting and looking far too handsome wearing a deep aubergine banyan and enticing half-smile.

"Good evening, ladies. How was Lady Pynes' ball?"

"Ever so lovely. I danced with Mr. Drinkwater and . . ." Jessica's words faded into the background as the gossip of her husband's infidelity echoed in Evelina's mind. She pulled her focus back to the moment to find Jessica still describing the other guests at the ball. "And then there was Mr. Gordon. His sister was present."

If Evelina did not interrupt, Jessica would probably recount the entire evening in precise detail, and she needed to speak with her husband. Now was as good as any time to confront him.

"It is getting late, Jessica, and tomorrow promises to be a full day." She then turned to her husband. "A word, in your study, Lord Raine." Evelina did not wait for a response but went to the room and waited for him to join her.

He followed in silence, entered the room, and closed the door, but all the while kept his distance and waited for her to speak.

Evelina crossed her arms, offering comfort to herself. "I heard some interesting information this evening."

"Oh?"

"About your whereabouts tonight."

"My whereabouts?" he questioned, his countenance giving nothing of his guilt away. "And where have I supposed to—"

"With Señora de la Barca," she stated with impatience. Why wouldn't he just admit his guilt? "I would appreciate you using more discretion when visiting your mistress and—"

"I do not have a mistress," he stated firmly.

"You were apparently seen in the arms of the opera singer." She stood her ground, wanting the truth. "Are you denying it?"

His gaze upon her was unwavering, his words firm and full of conviction. "I do not have a mistress. I have not spent time with an opera singer, or any woman in fact." He took a step closer. "I may be a lot of things, Evelina, but I gave you my word, and I do not lie. I will not dishonor—"

"But the rumors—"

"Are just that," he insisted once again.

"Then what have you been doing? You never attend any functions, and don't seem interested in Town."

"Because I detest Society." His words rang through the study, his confession taking her aback.

"But . . . but you're a rake and . . ." Evelina was more than a little confused. "And Lady Shephard said none of the Raine men have ever been faithful."

James let out a long sigh. "My father and his father before him were not." He took another step closer. "But I have been faithful to you." He took another step closer. "I will *not* dishonor our vows."

He was standing so close, too close.

Evelina did not know what to say. Why was he saying these things? Was he just playing with her emotions because he was desperate for an heir? She wanted to ask so many questions, but in the end, it was her husband who made the next move.

"It is getting rather late, and you are to host a ball tomorrow in Jessica's honor." And with that, he turned and left her once again.

Why did he always walk away from her?

# Chapter Nine

FRUSTRATION SEARED THROUGH James. He still hadn't recovered from the accusations his wife had hurled at him last evening—which he tried, with no success, not to care about. Then, of course, there was the guilt that had been simmering over not having attended any events with his wife this Season, not to mention the information he'd just received regarding the possible source of other rumors he had asked Lonsdale to uncover.

And now this.

The guests were due to arrive at any moment, his cousin was a nervous ball of feminine drama, but his wife was nowhere to be found. She wasn't with Jessica or in her private parlor or in any of the other places he'd looked. There was only one place left. He'd promised not to go to her room unless invited, but bedding his wife was not on his mind at the moment. There was much at stake this evening.

Taking the steps two at a time, he rushed up the stairs to the viscountess' suite, knocked, but when he didn't hear a response, opened the door. A soft hum drifted toward him followed by a gasp.

"Oh, my lord," her lady's maid said as she clutched the fabric of her dress about her chest, out of breath. "You startled me."

After scanning the room from the threshold and not seeing Evelina, he questioned, "Where's my wife?"

The woman took in a deep breath, then slowly said, "She is in the garden. She needed a moment and—"

"Thank you. That will be all," he said as he turned and left.

The garden. Hundreds of guests would soon be descending upon them and she went for a stroll? Did she have no regard for his cousin, or how this would make his family look? There were already plenty of rumors circulating about everything from his probable infidelity to hers. *Had she heard those rumors, too?* None of it was true, of course. But he didn't want it to affect Jessica, and he certainly didn't want to disappoint his aunt and uncle.

Servants cleared a wide path as he dashed through the house toward the gardens. The moment he stepped outside, coolness encircled him, easing the tension that had been consuming him a moment ago.

In the distance, down the torch-lit path, he spied Evelina. Her perfectly straight back was facing him, giving no hint of her mood. With long, consistent strides he went to where she was standing, but before he had a chance to remind her the guests were due to arrive at any moment, she spoke.

"I know my duty. I just needed a moment." Her voice was soft, strained, quavering.

Something didn't sit well. With caution, he approached, stepping in front of her. Her eyelids were puffy from crying. And then she looked into his eyes. The sadness he saw struck his heart.

He didn't know what to say. Once again, he wondered if she had heard the same gossip he had about their supposed mutual infidelity. Was she upset by those accusations, or was it something else? Did it have to do with this evening?

No. That didn't make sense. If Evelina was angry, she would certainly have let him know. Lord knew she'd done that plenty of times in recent weeks. No. This was something else.

As if reading his thoughts, she sniffled as she shook her head. "You needn't be concerned. I will be along shortly, my lord."

She started to turn from him, but he gently took her arm, holding her in place. "What's the matter?"

Those sad green eyes that in that moment reminded him of a drenched landscape on a rainy day met his gaze. He didn't know what he was expecting, but the sudden burst of tears followed by her collapsing into his embrace was surely the last thing.

As he held her something jarred his senses. He continued to hold her close, cradling her as she wept. Only once her breathing evened did he speak.

"What happened?" he said softly.

"I'm sorry. It's just that . . ." She sniffled, then shook her head and started to step out of his embrace.

A fierce protectiveness overtook him, demanding his attention, demanding he keep her close to him, to discover what had caused her to be so upset.

"Talk to me." It was probably the first he'd ever said such a thing to another. He never invited confidences. He never wanted to know what was wrong. And he certainly never wanted to share his own emotions. It was the best way to guard his heart. But here he was, wanting to know, waiting to know.

She was silent for several moments before finally speaking in *sotto voce*. "To—today is my mother's birthday and . . ." she swallowed hard, "and since Mama died, I've always spent this day with my sisters, sharing memories and . . ." She shook her head again. "I'm sorry, I—"

He cradled her face with one hand, wiping away a tear with his thumb. "Don't be sorry. I know I am a far cry from your sisters, but you can share with me." He offered a smile as he secretly hoped she would share even the tiniest part of her life with him.

He not only wanted to know about her interests, but he wanted to know about her, her life. He wanted to be part of her life, to share every moment with her.

She seemed shocked at his offer. "You want to know about my mother?" confusion laced her words.

"Yes." He couldn't explain beyond that simple three-letter word that held so much meaning.

Even while her lips curled into a half-smile, he could tell she was holding back the tears. "She was quite lovely and very . . . shall we say, determined at times."

"Now I know where you get that trait from," he teased gently, which brought a wider smile to her face. He wanted to make her smile like this every day.

Her eyes softened and James could feel the love she had for her family as she spoke of them. "My father encouraged all of us, including Mother, to explore our passions and never give up."

Guilt assailed him. Because of his actions, she had been forced to marry him to save her respectability when she should have been free to marry someone she loved, to explore her passion. But he hadn't wanted her to marry anyone else. He wanted her to be his and his alone. A deep internal sigh swept through him. She was his, but not truly. They shared no intimacies. Yes, he desired her, but there was more.

Her gaze was as soft as a caress, warm and inviting. Something shifted between them, something indefinable and not like anything he'd ever experienced. Did she sense it, too? Did she feel the same?

"Evelina—"

"Pardon me, Lord Raine," Martin said as he approached. "Your mother has arrived and would like a word with you." His tone suggested that Mother was none-too-pleased, which seemed about right for her.

James rolled his eyes heavenward. "Inform her that I will be there in a moment."

His butler nodded his head in understanding, then took his leave. Hopefully, his mother would not take her ire out on Martin.

James looked into Evelina's upturned face. "I hope you will share more of yourself in the future."

She offered a simple smile and a nod of her head. "Thank

you, James."

Evelina called him *James*. At that moment, his world seemed lighter. It was a good beginning.

THE GUESTS HAD arrived, the music was splendid, Jessica was enjoying herself and had many admirers, her mother-in-law was nowhere to be seen, and James . . .

Was never far from her side.

Every time their eyes met, his seemed to assess her, as if ensuring she was all right. It was both comforting and terrifying.

Evelina only ever shared her feelings with her sisters, but even then, not quite fully. She never wanted to appear weak. She wanted to be more like her dearest mama. Calm, in control, and ready to tackle any obstacle.

Tears stung the corners of her eyes and before she could blink them away, James was at her side. He didn't say anything, just offered his presence, which much to her surprise, was more comforting than words.

She didn't want to contemplate what that meant. It was easier to argue with him, to protect her heart, than to express what she felt.

"This is such a splendid party, Lord and Lady Raine," Lady Kirkwood said. It was a nice compliment coming from a premier hostess.

"My wife did indeed do a splendid job this evening and deserves all the credit, I assure you." Heat rushed to her cheeks with James' praise.

As the evening wore on, more guests offered compliments and congratulations on a perfect evening. Not that Evelina sought praise, but she hoped the success of the evening would waylay the current gossip.

Even the unfortunate arrival of Lady Mavis, who was in her

second Season and still had not secured a proposal despite being the daughter of a duke, could not put a damper on the evening. Evelina had hoped the rumormonger would stay away, but holding true to form, the woman seemed to fly in a flock with the other gossips, namely Miss Jerome. At least there was no fodder for them this evening.

By the time the guests had departed and Jessica retired, Evelina was experiencing a wide span of conflicting foreign emotions. As she trudged up the stairs, exhausted from the long evening entertaining, her mind wrestled with all that had occurred that day. Just as all previous nights, she went to her room alone, and just as all previous nights, James did not seek her out.

Since they'd married—since her mother first took ill, if she were being honest—Evelina had not quite felt herself. Until tonight. It had been a long time since she talked about her mother to anyone besides her sisters. She couldn't explain why, but sharing that part of her life with James was soothing.

His kindness earlier had meant a great deal to her, and she wanted him to know just how much it did.

Without further thought, she went to the door that joined their suites and knocked softly. She didn't know if this was the right course or best idea. Hesitation gurgled within and she started to turn away when the door opened, revealing her husband, still dressed in his evening attire.

"Evelina?" surprise laced the single word.

"I . . . I . . . I wanted to thank you for your kind words earlier, and . . ." She swallowed hard.

They both stood, staring at each other as if neither knew what to do. She certainly did not.

As he took a hesitant step forward, her pulse started to race, but not with fear.

*He is your husband. It would be perfectly acceptable to . . .*

She shook those thoughts away. She came to express her appreciation, not to succumb to seduction.

He stared at her for several seconds before he retreated. "You're most welcome." He sucked in a deep breath as he took another step back. "Good night, Evelina."

The sound of her name on his lips sent a ripple of desire all the way down to her toes. "Good night, James."

Then he closed the adjoining door, honoring his vow.

# Chapter Ten

J AMES HAD LAIN awake all night. How could he sleep when the object of his desire was in the next room? Something had changed between them and he was curious if she sensed it too. He'd enjoyed hearing about her family and wanted to know more. He just wanted to spend time with his wife.

As the sun rose, and it promised to be a pleasant day, James decided today was the day he would get to know his wife better. Perhaps she would be amenable to a ride in Hyde Park?

Hours later, his plan having come to fruition, he and his wife rode side by side, taking a gentle pace through the park. James could not remember the last time he'd enjoyed the company of the opposite sex out of bed this much. He felt at peace riding beside Evelina. She was an accomplished horsewoman.

"It is such a beautiful day," Evelina said. "It feels like ages since I last rode."

He'd often been curious how she spent her days while they were apart. "Did you ride often in the country?"

"Before my parents took ill, we frequently rode together." The tenderness in her voice whenever she spoke of her family stirred a deeper longing within him.

He could not ever remember having heard similar tenderness coming from either of his parents toward each other or anyone else. If he were being honest, most of his relatives—apart from his younger sister and cousin—never showed any affection toward each other. Only since his eldest sister, Henrietta, had become a mother had her countenance softened. And while growing up, although he'd adored his little sister, he'd always found Daisy's constant eavesdropping and dramatics more of an annoyance day to day than anything else. At least married life seemed to have tamed that tendency in her.

Then it dawned on him. "Did you not ride while at Raine Hall?"

She looked away for a moment, then responded, "Those are your horses. I didn't . . ."

He pulled Hermes to a stop, prompting her horse to do the same. "They're your horses, too. My homes are your homes." He didn't know what possessed him, but he added, "All that I have is yours."

She worried her lip, almost in embarrassment. "I didn't mean to imply I was lacking anything."

"I know." She'd never asked anything of him and yet he found himself wanting to give her all of himself. "Although our marriage did not begin in the most auspicious way, I do hope you—we—can find happiness."

He braced himself for an argument, for her to blame him again for the necessity of their marriage, for having to be in Town . . . for everything. But much to his surprise, she didn't. Quite the opposite, in fact.

"I do, too."

EVELINA'S DAY HAD begun so pleasantly with the morning ride in the park with James, but quickly deteriorated the moment they'd returned. She'd received a letter from Aunt Imogene that she would not be due back in Town for another week or two, then a note from Lady Dorothy—one of her dearest friends—who wanted to let her know that rumors were circulating about the Three Graces Salon, and had culminated a few hours later when Jessica was readying for the evening's soirée.

The sound of wailing filled the house, prompting Evelina and her lady's maid to run from her suite, dashing down the hall, nearly colliding with Jessica's lady's maid, who was practically in tears.

"What happened?" Evelina asked.

"Miss Raine was not pleased with how the bodice of the dress was sitting and then tried—"

"It's ruined!" Jessica's cry echoed down the hall.

"Perhaps I can fix the issue," Georgette, Evelina's lady's maid, said, as she headed toward the sound of wails.

The trio went to Jessica's room, where she was sitting at her dressing table, sobbing as though her heart were broken, a tear obvious on the front of her bodice.

"Dearest," Evelina soothed, hoping to calm her. "Georgette is quite talented with a needle, but you must stop crying."

She sniffled multiple times before her breathing evened. Only then did she nod her head in acquiescence. Although the tear was in a most inconvenient place, before long, Georgette had disguised the rip, and further agitation was averted.

If only all of life's problems were so easily fixed. No matter how hard Evelina tried, James was always on the edge of her thoughts, a constant conundrum.

By the time Jessica's dress was mended and they were ready to depart, Evelina was ready to retire. Her head ached with all the confusion that roiled within every time James was near. She desperately wished her sisters and Aunt Imogene were here to offer advice.

"You both look lovely this evening," James said as he descended the stairs. The sight of him in his evening attire nearly took her breath away.

"I didn't know you'd be joining us, James," Jessica said with excitement.

"I couldn't help myself," he offered with a wink.

There was something so different in his mannerisms. It was almost as if he wanted to go this evening, wanted to be with them. Evelina shook those thoughts away. It was likely just to allay further gossip, she was sure. He was doing this for his cousin, not for her.

Soon they were ensconced in the carriage and moving along at a gentle pace. Jessica had fully recovered from her earlier distress and was now talking nonstop about how much she was looking forward to seeing Mr. Drinkwater. Evelina did not know if James would object to the match. The young gentleman was the second son of baron, with only two thousand a year, but he was delightful and caring toward Jessica. She supposed that would be a topic of conversation for later.

The evening progressed as was expected. Refreshments, dancing, and of course much conversation over Lord Raine's presence. The moment he joined some of the other men for a game of cards, Evelina was swarmed with questions from various ladies. And then Lord Dougherty approached. She'd been trying to avoid the notorious scoundrel and gambler since her first Season.

"Good evening, Lady Raine," the silky words slithered from Lord Dougherty's mouth like a snake about to strike.

"Lord Dougherty," she said with a nod of her head.

She started to turn from him when he said, "I've heard numerous rumors that you're most unhappy with your current predicament." Whether she was happy or not was not his affair, and Evelina was about to tell him as much when he added, "Perhaps I could aid you in discovering your happiness."

The innuendo was loud and clear and completely disgusted her.

Evelina raised her chin, stared directly at him, and said, "I do not think you capable." And with that, she turned and walked away.

No sooner had she created distance from the undesirable rake, than Miss Kitty Ashton and two of her friends approached.

"Have you given any thought to what we discussed previously?" Miss Ashton questioned in a soft voice, clearly hopeful for news of the salon.

"Not much," Evelina had to admit.

All three of the young ladies let out a mutual sigh of disappointment, but it was Miss Dean who spoke. "Please say you'll change your mind. We have nowhere to discuss men and all the gossip this Season, especially the tidbits surrounding a particular woman caught in a compromising situation."

And therein lay the problem. Their salon hadn't been formed as a place simply to gather and spread salacious gossip, rather to discuss how to avoid certain trappings, not condemn compromised women but to discover how to not become one. Although the original intent of the salon was still valid, something had shifted. Perhaps it was she who had changed. Evelina couldn't explain exactly what had changed, only that her purpose in life was different now.

Not wanting to give the trio false hope, she simply offered a little wisdom. "Ignore the gossip, and keep a trusted circle of friends."

Though the evening had hardly begun, it already felt like hours had passed. All Evelina wanted to do was forget about Lord Dougherty's inappropriateness, forget about all the comments swirling, and find a dim corner and have a quiet moment of peace.

With the dancing having begun, and Jessica preoccupied with Mr. Drinkwater, she seized the opportunity. She ventured down the hall with the hope of stealing a moment in the ladies' retiring room when a familiar deep voice called to her.

"We seem to meet often in such circumstances," James teased.

She wasn't sure what came over her, but Evelina was suddenly feeling quite bold, her previous woes dissipating under a wave of tingles. "Are you going to accuse me of trying to seduce you again?" she asked archly.

"Always." The single word was deep and far too enticing.

Her mouth went dry and she struggled to find words. Thankfully, Lady Fanny's high-pitched laughter echoed down the hall, breaking the spell.

"I . . . I should return to your cousin," she said as she scurried away.

The remainder of the evening passed in slow measures. Once again, when they returned home, James retired to his room, Evelina's to hers.

With each passing day, she found herself becoming more and more curious about her husband. There was still only one problem: she wasn't prepared to succumb without love.

EVELINA DID NOT wish ill upon Jessica. However, she was glad for a reprieve from social obligations, and was looking forward to an evening in their residence. She longed for the quiet of the country, the calm star-filled nights, and brisk mornings full of hope. But those longings would have to wait for another day. Tonight, she was to dine with her husband.

And she was nervous. Nervous and, truth be told, a little excited.

Evelina surveyed her image in the mirror once again. The violet lace dress accentuated her curves. Would James notice? Did she even want him to notice?

*He's a rake.* That refrain was getting rather tiresome, particularly as even she could admit he hadn't been acting particularly rakish.

*He's also your husband.* And that argument with herself was also getting rather tiresome. If only there were some clear sign that her heart would be safe with him and she could have all that she desired.

The clock began to chime. It was time to dine with her husband. With each step she took, nervous excitement coursed faster through her veins and the butterflies in her stomach soared. What would they talk about?

She stopped on the threshold, overcome by the sight of James standing near the fireplace, his blond hair shimmering in the soft light, looking far too seductive by far. In that moment, she felt . . . lacking.

"Good evening, Evelina," he said as he went to her side, then offered his arm. "Shall we?"

The moment her ungloved hand rested on his firm, muscular forearm, Evelina knew she would have trouble focusing. As they strolled toward the dining room, she attempted to create a list of topics they could talk about, but all she could think about was the incredibly handsome man at her side. She inhaled, taking in his masculine scent, relishing in the strength he projected. What would it be like to be wrapped in his arms and—

*Stop!*

And to be kissed by him again, to feel his hands . . .

*No! Stay strong and do not be beguiled.*

And the argument in her head started once again, heat-inducing wonderings interspersed with firm commands to concentrate.

By the time she'd been seated in the room, Evelina thought she would melt from all her inappropriate thoughts.

"Is my cousin feeling better?"

Cousin? Oh, yes, Jessica! So wrapped up in her thoughts, she'd almost forgotten why they'd stayed in this evening.

"Slightly. She informed me that her megrims can sometimes last for several days." Evelina wasn't about to go into more detail about what his cousin suffered from. Some things were better left unsaid. "She's quite upset over the prospect of missing Lady Livingstone's grand ball three days hence."

"Ah, yes, Lady Livingstone's ball. It is *the* event of the Season.

I'm certain the fashions will be exquisite," he teased. "What color do you think Lady Jerome will wear this year? And of equal importance, who will rival her fashion sense?"

Evelina was enjoying this playful side of James. "I'm certain Lady Gordon's colorful feathered plumes will be the highlight of the event," she said with a giggle, remembering said lady's ball a few weeks ago where her headpiece towered above her head, almost at a tipping point. "I only hope she refrains from the eau de jasmine."

"Do you not care for the scent?"

She scrunched her nose. "Not at all. It is my sister-in-law's favorite and . . ." She shook her head, trying to find more subtle words to describe the effect Rachel had on her and her sisters.

"You needn't say more." He eyed her for a moment before taking a sip of wine. She watched as the deep red liquid touched his lips. *Oh my, but it was getting warm in here.* And then he spoke, and her insides melted even further. "What scent do you prefer?"

He wanted to know something specifically about her?

She thought for a moment. "Spring on a clear day, lavender after the rain, autumn as the leaves change color, and—"

James' pleasant chuckle filled the room. "That is quite poetic."

"I do have an affinity for poetry."

"I will have to remember that," he said with a half-smile that sent her pulse racing anew. He seemed quite genuine in his attempt to know her better this evening.

They dined in a relaxed atmosphere and when dinner came to an end, Evelina decided to stay while James took his brandy.

"Would you care for a glass?" he asked.

She knew he was just being polite, but she had taken brandy once before with him, so he shouldn't be too shocked by her acceptance. "That would be lovely." James didn't say a word, but took a glass from the side table and poured her a small helping. She took the offered glass, then raised it to her lips and inhaled the spicy scent and took a sip. "Why is it only men can drink brandy and it not be deemed improper?"

The spot between his brow crinkled for a moment, then relaxed as he spoke. "I suppose it is because the fairer sex does not have the constitution for such strong spirits, and their reputations could be compromised."

"I'm of the fairer sex and I enjoy a glass of brandy in the evening," she pointed out.

"You, my dear, have a strong constitution."

*My dear.* She didn't know if it were his words or the brandy, but suddenly Evelina felt very over-heated, lightheaded even. She brought a hand to her cheek but found no relief.

*Oh, dear, but what was James about this evening?*

Without so much as a warning, he pushed back from the table and stood. "Would you care to play a game of billiards?"

Never one to back down, Evelina stood and met his gaze. "It would be a pleasure."

He waved a hand. "After you."

She led the way toward the game room. She could sense him following close behind. How could she not? Her hands ached to touch, her body to be touched. *Why did he have this power over her?*

As she entered the room, then picked up a stick, she inquired, "The rules?"

"Cue end to strike, two points for sinking the cue ball, three for the red." He took a step closer to her. "A wager?"

Evelina was confident in her abilities. She'd played against her siblings often enough and always won. What did she have to lose? "Yes."

The words rolled off his tongue as if they were most common. "If I win, we play *Le Baiser a la Capucine.*"

*Kiss of the Monkey?* Certainly, monkeys could not be involved.

"I am not familiar with that game."

"All the better for me." His sly tone was suggestive and she could guess the result of winning that game.

"*And,*" she began with emphasis, "if *I* win, you shall keep your distance." But even as she said the words, she did not believe that was what she truly wanted.

He countered her wager, upping the stakes. "*If* you win, I shall retire to the country for the remainder of the Season."

For the second time that evening, Evelina wondered what he was up to, but did she truly not want him around? Doubt over what she wanted settled into her gut.

"Agreed," she responded with some reluctance.

With every strike she took, she could feel James' eyes on her, watching. And not on the game. She was finding it difficult to concentrate. And when James took his stance, bending slightly as he assessed the angle for his shot, she could not help but stare at his magnificent form. What would he look like without his clothes on? Would his muscles tense and flex with each movement?

"And that's a game," James announced bringing her out of reflections.

What had just happened?

She'd lost! How did she lose?

She didn't know how to play *Le Baiser a la Capucine*, or even what it was exactly, but she was most certain she was not going to like it.

James strolled up to her with all the confidence of an experienced rake. Her mouth suddenly felt dry, her hands moist, and her heart . . . oh dear, it was pounding so hard in her chest she thought all of London may hear it.

"You need to go down on your knees," the silky words brushed past his lips.

"Pardon?" She swallowed hard. "My knees?"

He offered a half-smile as he nodded. "Sit back on your heels."

Evelina lifted her skirt slightly, then did as he said. James circled around her, then with his back to hers, went down on his knees, pressing his back to hers. The warmth of him took her breath away. What was he doing to her?

"Give me your hands."

And once again, without even the slightest hesitation, she did as she was told. The moment their ungloved hands touched, something electric passed between them. She tilted her head to the right to see if he'd felt it, too, but was met with a kiss. The caress of his lips on her mouth brought back remembrances of their first kiss, their only kiss. Desire and need shot through her.

Evelina was wrong. She was enjoying this interlude too much—far too much.

She shifted her body, wanting to feel more of him, and then in the next breath, the kiss ended.

James stood, then helped her to her feet. "It would be best for you to retire." And as was becoming his wont, he left the room, leaving her standing, wanting more, more of him.

# Chapter Eleven

"ARE YOU FEELING any better today?" Evelina asked Jessica as she entered the warm, dark room.

"Not really," Jessica sniffled. A moment later, she burst into tears. "I'm missing the entire Season! All the balls and musicales, and the dances . . ." Jessica continued to sob uncontrollably, wailing about everything she was missing out on.

"Oh, dearest," Evelina soothed as she went to Jessica's bedside and smoothed the tangled strands of hair off her damp face. "Don't cry. It cannot be good for your megrim." Jessica breathed in and out in huge breaths as she sniffled, trying to still her breathing. Once she was calmer, Evelina attempted to ease her concerns. "You won't miss the entire Season, just a few days. I assure you, it is not as awful as you believe, and before long, you'll be good as new and dancing once again."

Evelina could hear the heartache in each word Jessica spoke. "But . . . but what if Mr. Drinkwater finds someone else?"

She wasn't an expert in this area. Far from it. She'd never had the opportunity to form any sort of an attachment, to be wooed. "Then it wasn't meant to be," Evelina said, hoping the simple explanation was all that was needed.

"How did you know that my cousin was your heart's true desire?" Jessica asked with a dreamy smile.

Oh dear, how was she to respond?

Evelina couldn't very well shatter the young girl's fantasy. Just because her marriage was not what she'd hoped for, that didn't mean that Jessica should not find love and happiness. Jessica continued to sit in hopeful anticipation of a romantic story. Evelina thought back to the beginning, to the first time she'd first laid eyes on him, to the times when she and James were at the same functions, in the same room, and then the words started to pour from her mouth as if of their own accord.

"I suppose it was the way he looked at me. Subtle glances from across the room, the way his eyes followed me, watched me. And then . . . when he spoke. His deep, melodic voice . . ." her words trailed off and the butterflies in her stomach fluttered rapidly as if trying to escape and be free, free to explore, to explore the passion that had been simmering between her and James since the very beginning. She shook her head, trying to push away those thoughts. "You should probably get some rest. I'll check on you later."

Evelina did not wait for Jessica to respond but quickly dashed from the room. A nervousness coursed through her veins that she could not contain. But just as she closed the door to Jessica's room, she came face to face with the man who had just been disturbing her thoughts and stirring desire.

"How is my cousin?" Although his words were laced with concern for his relative, his eyes—his delicious chocolate brown eyes—were centered on her, as if he'd just been reading her thoughts.

Heat flared in her cheeks and all words escaped her for a moment before she regained some semblance of her senses. "Better. She still may need a day or two before she can venture out again. She's worried about missing the Season, but I told her these things take time." Evelina went from barely being able to speak to rambling. What was wrong with her?

"Then that will give us some time together."

Evelina swallowed hard, then whispered, "Time together?"

James took a step in, his maleness surrounding her, distracting her. "It's a beautiful day." He held out his arm. "Shall we?"

She supposed she could deny him, but something deep down urged her to accept. She was tired of the warring and avoiding, and they'd really been getting on quite well lately. And besides, it was perfectly acceptable to enjoy a day out with one's husband. With her mind made up, she placed a hand on his arm. "I would be delighted."

Before long they were stepping out of the house and into the bright day. The elegant carriage was awaiting their departure.

"Are you ready for an adventure?" he asked as he handed her into the conveyance.

"Where are we going?"

"You will just have to wait and see," he responded enigmatically.

In that moment, James seemed less like a rake and more like a gentleman with no ulterior motive other than just enjoying the company of another. Evelina wondered if this was truly who he was or if it was for show, simply part of his repertoire. She looked into his eyes and knew it was the former.

Soon they were leaving Town, and the pace of the world around them seemed to slow. Evelina glanced over at James. The worry lines that constantly framed his brown eyes had disappeared. Just like the gentle breeze and playful clouds dotting the sky, he seemed more relaxed, at ease. Even the corners of his lips held the hint of a smile. Those lips that created the scandal of the Season *and* brought sensations she'd never felt.

"What are you thinking?" his question brought her out of her musings of him.

Heat rushed to her cheeks. She couldn't very well tell him that she'd been thinking about his lovely lips and the kiss they'd shared last evening. She cleared her throat. "Just about the passing scenery. It is quite lovely."

Thankfully he did not seem to suspect the direction of her thoughts, but simply agreed with her assessment. "It is quite refreshing being out of the city, and away from the crush of the *ton*, prying eyes, and expectations."

His remark took her aback. She'd always assumed that he enjoyed the city. "Expectations?"

"Expectations." A frustrated sigh escaped his lips. "The expectation that I will achieve something great, but all the while fostering doubt in every aspect of life and over every decision." He looked at her and their gazes locked. "But what everyone is truly waiting for, watching for, is something to gossip about. All eyes watching, waiting for you to make a mistake or create a scandal."

The words escaped her mouth before she could stop them. "It seems to me that you excel at creating scandals."

Laughter, deep masculine laughter, filled the carriage. "I assure you, it wasn't always by choice." His features turned serious, solemn almost. There was a longing tinged with sadness in his eyes that made her pause. There was so much more to her husband than she'd first assumed. How had she not seen it before? She was beginning to suspect that inside, he was just a simple man wanting to provide for his family, his tenants, and live a peaceful life. "Stirring gossip of *my* choosing deflected attention from my shortcomings."

*Shortcomings.* When Evelina's father had first taken ill, coming in and out of reality, he'd feared that his faults, his shortcomings, would be his family's undoing. As the disease progressed, his worries and concerns grew. Did James have similar worries?

"And what shortcomings might those have been?" As she said the words, she watched him closely.

His voice lowered to just above a whisper. "That I wasn't good enough . . ." He shook his head as the words trailed off.

*Oh dear, Papa had felt the same.*

A moment later, he tried to change the subject. "I suppose my cousin will be well enough to attend the upcoming musicale."

Evelina reached out and touched his hand, wanting to offer comfort, understanding, as indeed he had done for her. His gaze shifted to where their two hands met. "James," she softly said his name. "Talk to me."

He closed his eyes as he shook his head. His breathing increased as he seemed to fight some distant memory.

"Please."

When he finally spoke, his words were quiet. "That I wasn't good enough for the viscountcy."

"Who would say such—"

"My father, grandfather, but especially my mother . . ." he shook his head as if trying to erase the past. It was clear that he was not able to share all, not now, that whatever happened had caused him great distress. She hoped with time, he would open up to her more. But this was a start.

She placed her other hand on his arm, desperate to comfort him, defend him. "You *are* good enough, and the viscountcy *is* flourishing." She knew her statement to be the absolute truth.

Her many months in the country at Raine Hall had shown her just how responsible he was. Every aspect of the estate ran smoothly and that was a testament to the man sitting beside her. There was no doubt in her mind that James did all he could for the sake of family and title.

JAMES LOOKED DOWN at Evelina's hand. Searing desire and something else—some foreign emotion mingled and collided with want. What the hell was happening to him? Never in his life had he opened up to another soul, nor had he ever wanted to. And now, an intense desperation to share his very existence filled him.

*Emotions are for the weak and will only serve to destroy your life.* His grandfather's words echoed in his mind.

He clenched his jaw and inhaled deeply, as he fought to push those imprudent words from his mind.

Evelina glanced out the window as the carriage slowed and stopped. Thankfully, she seemed distracted by their location. "Where are we?"

"Sweet Briar Manor." James opened the door to the conveyance and stepped down, then turned and assisted Evelina. The moment he took her hands in his hand, he felt at peace, as if this was where he was meant to be. "While you were at Raine Hall, this is where I was."

He could hear the shock in her tone. "You didn't stay in Town?"

"This may come as a surprise, but I do not care for Town. Although I am not fond of long walks, I much prefer the quiet of the country." *Damn.* He cursed himself as the confession poured from his mouth as if of its own accord.

And then she asked the single question that disrupted his entire being. "Why do you not care for walks?"

He ignored the question. "The picnic is waiting for us."

Evelina stepped in front of him and looked into his eyes. He started to look away when she said his name with such tenderness that he could deny her nothing in that moment. "James, please."

"Walks in the country were synonymous with letting my sire down. When I was a child, the only time he'd spend with me was on long walks where he would lecture, dictate, and order my course of activities." *And sometimes strike me.* But he would not reveal that pain to her. He could not.

A gentle hand cupped his cheek. "Perhaps we can change that," she said as she intertwined her arm with his. "To take away some of those hurts."

And with her words, his world became brighter. How was it possible that one woman could ease past sufferings with simple words? Though it wasn't just words, was it? It was how she made him feel, that he *was* good enough.

Soon they were enjoying the picnic feast laid before them. The pigeon pie, gingerbread cakes, and almond raisin apple puffs were delicious, the company perfect, and the day inspirational. James could not remember the last time he'd enjoyed an outing such as this. More importantly, he was pleased to just be enjoying this time with Evelina and didn't want it to end. And wanted to share more of himself.

Whenever he was at Sweet Briar Manor, he liked to visit his tenants. He hoped she would enjoy it as well. "After lunch, I thought we could visit the tenants before heading back. I instructed baskets to be readied."

Her bright smile said all he needed to know. "I would enjoy that very much."

Baskets had been prepared and loaded into the waiting carriage, and his heart gave a fierce thud against his chest as he handed her in as well. She was positively radiant and seemed excited for the outing.

Before long, they were delivering baskets. He watched Evelina interact with the various tenant wives. Apart from their clothing and manner of speech, one would never guess the difference in station. His wife had a way about her that made people comfortable.

*His wife.* Pride bubbled within. Evelina was a natural. The tenants adored her, especially the children. Would they ever have a child of their own? The thought startled him. For the first time in his life, he did not think about an heir, but a child. A child to teach the way of the land to. A child to love.

THE DAY HAD been most lovely. Evelina had enjoyed herself more than she was willing to admit. The anger that had been consuming her over the scandal he'd stirred had dissipated and the more he revealed of himself, the more attracted to him she found herself. She still didn't entirely understand why he'd kissed her, but at least they weren't arguing anymore.

The ride back to the city passed in pleasant conversation about the various tenants she'd met and improvements James had already completed and those he'd been planning. Soon, they were back in town, and discussing the next events.

"And this evening we are to dine . . ." His words trailed off as he caught sight of something outside the carriage.

Evelina followed his gaze, then the carriage came to an abrupt halt. *Lady Raine.* Her mother-in-law was standing on the front steps, hands on hips, glaring in their direction.

Why was she here?

James had only taken one step from the carriage when his mother demanded, "James. A word." As James approached Lady Raine, she heard her say, rather loudly, "I've received some unfortunate information about a certain lord and a soirée, and another tidbit I wish to discuss with you."

James offered an apologetic glance toward Evelina before guiding his mother into the house. She suspected it would not be a pleasant visit, and if Lady Raine held true to form, the older woman would probably place blame for whatever had occurred at Evelina's feet.

Doubt settled into her thoughts.

*Had* something occurred with Jessica at one of the functions? Evelina had watched her closely and hadn't seen anything untoward. It was probably just more gossip aimed at causing Evelina and James grief.

But she couldn't worry about that at the moment. There were other things that required her full attention.

# Chapter Twelve

A SENSE OF calm washed over Evelina as she watched the sky turn from vibrant pink to deep rose. It was the end of another beautiful day. She'd very much enjoyed walking in the garden, stopping to smell the roses, and reading poetry under the great oak tree. She cherished days such as these when there were few, if any, social obligations and Lady Raine—James' mother—was not intruding in their home and insisting on a word with her son, as she had the day before. Evelina had even had the opportunity to write lengthy letters to both her sisters and Aunt Imogene. Although she still missed them, of course, she could also sense a new existence was beginning to blossom.

Jessica was still indisposed, which meant one more quiet evening in, and that suited Evelina just fine. Soon her young ward would be right as rain and ready to tackle the Season once again, and then there would be no more calm afternoons or peaceful evenings.

"Lady Raine, pardon the interruption, but Lord Raine asked that I give this to you," one of the downstairs maids said as she approached, then handed Evelina a folded note, before quickly retreating to the house.

She glanced down at the paper. In fanciful, yet masculine writing were the words "Lady Raine."

*Lady Raine.*

She'd been married to James for nearly eight months, and plenty of people had spoken her new title, but seeing his script on the paper made it feel so much more real. In the past weeks, things had shifted between them. The arguments were few, and instead they talked about their days, their likes and dislikes, and even about their families.

It was almost like they were becoming friends.

She unfolded the paper and began to read.

*From time to time, one needs to dance. So, if you are inclined to prance, join me in the ballroom at the chime of seven.*

Laughter bubbled within at James' attempt at poetry. Oh dear, a poet he was not, but she appreciated the attempt and found it most endearing.

They had no plans to attend any events or entertain at home this evening, and James had told her that he did not particularly enjoy dancing, so she presumed his words must have a different meaning, but what that might be she could not discern. She was quite confused but supposed she could wait a couple of hours to discover what he was up to.

At ten minutes to seven, Evelina ventured toward the ballroom. She had been curious all afternoon, but as she entered the grand space, she was not prepared for what James had actually done.

The soft sounds of music drifted across the space. Off to one side, partially hidden by pedestals topped with roses was a quartet of musicians. The large space was reduced to an intimate circle surrounded by several decorative screens and even more flowers, creating an air of quiet and privacy.

James stepped out from behind one of the screens that had painted on it a scene of classical Rome. "Good evening, Lady Raine," his warm deep voice enticed her, stirring a need at her very core.

"What is all this?"

"You once accused me of not liking to dance." He held out

his hand, waiting for her to accept the unspoken invitation. "I am here to inform you that you are quite incorrect." As she accepted his hand, he drew closer, towering above her. "I simply do not like dancing with other women." He leaned in, the scent of soap and male invading her senses. "I only want to dance with my wife." His words brushed across her cheek, creating a torrent of tingles that reached all the way down to her toes.

Evelina was speechless. She pulled back and looked into his rich chocolate-colored eyes and saw the desire that always seemed to be lingering there, but she also saw something more.

Just then, the music crescendoed, and James began to guide her through a waltz. As their bodies drew closer, she could feel the heat emanating from him, surrounding her. It was a magical, sensual moment.

"Why did you do all this?" The words exited her mouth on a breathy whisper.

"I want to prove to you that there is more to me than what you assume." The rise and fall of his chest and his quiet words suggested he was nervous.

But the rumors, his past reputation as a rake, and his desire to have an heir still played in her mind. Would those concerns ever ease? She challenged his words. "So, you're not trying to seduce me to get what you want?"

"No." The single word was firm and full of conviction.

"Oh . . . I . . ."

"I swear on all your poetry books combined that I want nothing more this evening than to dance with my wife."

"That is quite the promise." She may not know everything about her husband, but she was certain that he was a man of his word.

"And one I won't break."

No further words were spoken as he held her in his arms and guided her through the sensual dance. Evelina now understood why so many mamas objected to this particular dance. There was an intimacy in the maneuvers that seemed almost inappropriate, but in the arms of her husband felt entirely exquisite.

When the music faded, James kept his promise. He did not press his advantage during dinner, or when they took brandy after, or even when they waltzed one last time. He was a perfect gentleman.

"Thank you for the enchanting evening, Lady Raine." And just as on previous occasions, they retired to their separate quarters, only this time, she wished they hadn't.

THE NEXT DAY, Jessica was recovered, and more than excited to reenter Society. Evelina, on the other hand, could not wait for the Season to end so she could escape the incessant gossip that seemed only to increase as the Season progressed. Although she had not been named specifically in the gossip sheets, the latest round implied that a woman who was forced last Season to marry a rake had recently been seen in the arms of another.

Evelina was certainly in no mood to endure Lady Wyner's ball this evening, especially without James—who had been summoned by his mother in regard to an unnamed, urgent matter—but duty had called, and here she was, watching her ward dance with Mr. Drinkwater. But all the while she was wondering who was behind these vicious attacks on her reputation, however oblique they remained.

Was it Lady Shephard, whose tongue was constantly wagging? Or perhaps Lady Jerome or her daughter, who always seemed to be the first to know new gossip? She scanned her memory, thinking back to her first Season when Alexandra and Theodora were also navigating the *ton*, and to those who were most against them.

Her ponderings were interrupted by the arrival of her friend Lady Neave, née Miss O'Donnell. "I need to speak with you," she said as she glanced about, then pulled Evelina toward a less crowded corner. "I was in the ladies retiring room and overheard your name mentioned."

"Mine? By whom?"

"Yes, by Lady Archibald. She said she'd heard it on good authority that you had a clandestine liaison with a particular rake who also has a gambling problem, and that Lord Raine, so upset, sought solace with his mistress."

She fumed with anger. Who would dare spew such bile? Anyone who truly knew her would know she would never cuckold her husband, regardless of how the marriage started, and James had sworn he had no mistress. "I would never—"

"Of course not!" Lady Neave glanced about, then said, "And she stated that Lord Raine discovered the interlude and is going to call the man out."

How did Lady Archibald know so many details of this outlandish story? Evelina needed to get to the bottom of this. She was tired of being dragged through the gossip sheets on an almost daily basis.

"Do you know when this will supposedly happen?"

"Tonight. That is why Lord Raine is in attendance this evening."

Her husband was in attendance? When had he arrived, and why hadn't he searched her out? Could he believe the rumors to be true?

Shock laced her words. "James is here?"

"Yes!" her friend exclaimed, startling those nearest them.

"I need to find James," the words rushed from Evelina's mouth as she glanced about looking to see if her husband was in the ballroom.

Lady Neave put a comforting hand on Evelina's arm. "Do not worry about Miss Raine. I will chaperone her for the remainder of the evening and ensure she returns home safely. You go find your husband."

"Thank you." It was good to have trusted friends who not only came to one's aid without hesitation, but also thought of the details one hadn't yet considered.

"You're most welcome. Now *go*."

Evelina needed no further encouragement as she strategically maneuvered through the ballroom. Damn, he wasn't here.

She then searched the refreshment hall and card room, but there was still no sign of James. Had she missed him? And then she spied James escorting another man down one of the side galleries. Careful not to be seen, she followed them.

As she neared the dark room, she heard a loud *thwack*. She rushed into the room to see James standing over a man in fine evening attire.

JAMES WAS LIVID. No, livid was too mild a word. First he'd had his mother's summons, which turned out to be nothing more than her wanting to air her displeasure with him once again, then he'd received a message from Lonsdale that Lord Dougherty was spreading a wild tale about Evelina. He went to his club, expecting to confront the blackguard at one of his known haunts, but he'd already left for Lady Wyner's event. Without thought for the consequences, he followed him here.

The moment he saw him—cajoling some young miss—anger boiled to the surface. He stormed to the rakehell's side. "A word."

Not giving him a chance to protest or run, James pushed him along at a close distance down a side gallery and into an unused room.

"What the hell is this all about?" Dougherty demanded.

James' answer came in the full force of his fist making contact with Dougherty's face, whose head whipped back. He doubled over just as Evelina rushed into the room.

*Damn.* He hadn't meant for Evelina to witness this outburst. First, he had to deal with Dougherty, then he would ease his wife's concerns.

James took a step closer to the scum, grabbing his cravat, he raised him up to his feet, then said, "And if I ever hear even a whisper from you about my wife, you won't have to worry about being called out."

Even in the dim light, James could see the fear in Dougherty's eyes.

*Good.* The rakehell should fear his wrath.

Holding his hand to his jaw, Dougherty turned on his heel and fled the room without a word.

Evelina went to James' side. Although her face was hidden in shadow, the concern in her voice was clear. "Are you all right? What happened?"

Frustrated, James ran a hand through his hair. This was not the time or place to discuss such delicate matters, but Evelina deserved an explanation, albeit a brief one. For the moment at least.

"Your honor was at stake."

"My honor?" Her voice rose slightly. "I don't understand. You were willing to call a man out and risk your life to defend my honor, and why? Because you heard a whisper?"

"Damn it, Evelina. You're my wife!" He would defend his own no matter the consequence. "I am responsible for you, and although you didn't want this marriage, I know that you would never dishonor our vows. I will not have anyone claiming otherwise."

Evelina clamped her lips tight. *Dammit.* He hadn't meant to be harsh, but the gossip, the desire he felt for her, the desire to be near her was all too much for one man to bear. He took a step closer, and that same electricity that always seemed to be present charged through him again.

"Evelina . . . I . . . ." Loud laughter erupted from down the hall, breaking the moment. He backed away. "Will we ever have even a moment?" he asked, mostly to himself as he ran his hand through his hair again. "Come on, we should return to the ball."

"I don't want to return. I want to know what happened, and

not some vague excuse. I want to know the whole truth. The truth about your—"

"Is anything the matter?" Lady Shephard's voice called from the open doorway. "I saw Lord Dougherty and assumed—"

"Assumed what?" James' harsh words challenged her to finish the sentence she pretended to be too delicate to complete.

The woman was clearly afraid. That made two people for the evening, but James didn't care. He had stood by long enough while rumormongers spread their wild tales. This would end tonight.

"Nothing. Nothing at all, Lord Raine."

# Chapter Thirteen

DESPITE LADY NEAVE offering to chaperone Jessica the rest of the evening, it wasn't necessary. After Lady Shephard interrupted their conversation, James decided it was time to leave. He quickly found Jessica, and before long, they were traveling back home.

Although Jessica's vibrant ramblings about what a wonderful evening it had been filled the carriage, the tension between Evelina and James was palpable. Thankfully, Jessica didn't seem to take notice, and once back at the house, she practically floated up to her room, humming a soft tune.

Evelina and James must have had the same thought, for Jessica had no more than reached the top of the stairs before they both went to the study. There was much to discuss, and Evelina would not rest until James told her everything.

No sooner had he shut the door, than all the thoughts that had been roiling within her surfaced. "You constantly tell me that rumors are just that, but at every event, in every scandal sheet, your name is mentioned and veiled references are made to me, and now even my name is on the gossips' lips, or so I heard this evening before you arrived." She paced the length of the room, then turned and stopped directly in front of him. "And then you call Lord Dougherty out!"

"I didn't call him out, I merely threatened—"

"Lord Raine, I appreciate that you say you have been faithful since we married—"

"I have been faithful since the day we met." He closed the distance but did not touch her. "I have not wanted to be near another woman, to touch another woman, to . . ." His words trailed off as he lowered his head, his warm intoxicating breath brushing across her cheek. "To kiss another woman."

Evelina closed her eyes, waiting for the kiss that seemed so near, but he took a step back. She opened her eyes to find him flush with desire—or perhaps in frustration.

"Damn it, Evelina." He ran a trembling hand through his hair. "You have seduced me mind, body, and soul. I made a promise to you that I would not come to you, that I would wait. But at every turn—"

*Knock, knock, knock.*

"Pardon me—"

"Is there no privacy in this house?" he exclaimed. He sucked in a deep breath as he clenched his fists tight. "I apologize Martin."

The butler looked from James to Evelina, then back to James, his cheeks red with embarrassment. "No apology needed, my lord. Your mother has arrived and has requested a word with you."

"At this hour? What the bloody hell? Wasn't once tonight enough?" he murmured as he ran his hand again through his already tousled hair.

James looked at her, so many emotions in those deep brown eyes, but didn't say a word. Then over his shoulder, he addressed the butler. "Thank you. I will deal with my mother straightaway."

Evelina watched as he left the room. She was tired of constantly watching him leave. She wanted . . .

*Dammit,* she didn't quite know what she wanted, but she knew she needed him.

HOURS LATER AND James had still not retired to his rooms. Was he angry with her? Was it true that he had not sought the comfort of a mistress since they'd met? Evelina may never have been intimate with her husband, but she was not entirely naïve. She knew that men had needs, that they sought pleasure where it was available. But if his claims were true, how then, did her husband satisfy those urges if not with a mistress? And what of all the rumors about him? Who was circulating those?

Evelina didn't know if he was still in the residence, but she did know, without a doubt, that she would not be able to sleep until she spoke with him. Once again, she found herself desperately needing answers. Tonight.

She knocked softly on his chamber door, but there was no answer. Grabbing her robe, she left her room. Since he wasn't in his room, she knew he would be in his study if he was in the house at all.

The house was quiet, almost eerie, as she padded down the halls. The night never bothered her, but there was something about this place that she found unsettling, even in the daylight hours, truth be told. She couldn't quite put her finger on why, but she suspected it had something to do with James' mother. Her presence seemed to linger even when she was not present.

She shook those thoughts away. This wasn't about Lady Raine. This was about her and James. Ever since that evening when he'd found her crying in the garden before the ball, something had begun to truly shift between them. And with each passing day, they seemed more at ease with each other. Until tonight.

As she approached the study, she noticed the door slightly ajar, the faint glow of candlelight spilling into the hall.

*He's home.*

She went to the door, knocked softly, then entered the warm

space. James was seated at his desk, staring at the open ledger, deep in concentration. The moment he looked up and their eyes met, his features softened.

"Evelina," he uttered her name with surprise and confusion. She supposed she couldn't blame him. She'd only searched him out once before.

After closing the door, she moved farther into the room. She didn't know quite what to say, or how to start, but decided to let her heart speak first. "I wanted to apologize—"

"There's no need. I shouldn't have lost my temper. It's just . . . I'm just . . ." Closing his eyes, he sucked in a deep breath as he shook his head. "Perhaps it's best that you retire."

Why was he pushing her away again? And before she could silence the thought, she blurted, "I don't want to retire. I want to understand."

"Understand what?" he grumbled as he stood.

"You say you haven't been with a woman since we met, but you're an admitted rake."

"What does that have—"

"Rakes want women, women who can please them. Rakes have needs." Heat rose in her cheeks as she spoke the next words. "Sexual needs. And rakes certainly—"

"How do you know about such . . ." He chuckled as realization dawned on him. "Ah yes, the salon you hosted with your sisters."

She stomped her foot in a most unladylike fashion. "Don't laugh." She was tired of being made to feel small or like she didn't deserve to know about men and the world. And they may not have a real marriage, but she had certainly tried to hold up her end of their deal and—at least in the eyes of the *ton*—be the perfect wife, the ideal viscountess. Could he not at least respect that?

"I may not have fulfilled your needs, but I'm trying to be the perfect viscountess."

He rounded the desk and closed the distance—but only slightly. "I don't want you to be the perfect viscountess. I just want you to be my wife."

Evelina was tired of this back and forth, tired of ignoring what she felt every time he was near. And then it struck her. All his kind words and subtle actions had been leading her to this. It was as if one of Eros' arrows had struck her heart and she was seeing, truly seeing, James for the first time. Recollections of moments of their time together caressed her thoughts. For so long, too long, she'd been fighting what she truly felt, afraid of what she felt. He may not feel the same, but perhaps with time he would. Was one-sided love enough to build a marriage, a lifetime?

*Love?*

*Dammit.* She'd fallen in love with her husband. The realization was as sudden as it was all-consuming, and it left her breathless.

James had said all along that he would not come to her, that he would wait for her. Well, *she* had said all along that she required love. And now she'd found it, at least in her own heart.

She knew her course forward. Tonight, she would come to him.

Evelina's heart pounded faster with each breath she took as she closed the distance between them. She placed a gentle hand on his chest, feeling his heart pounding just as hard as hers. His eyes turned dark with desire, encouraging her to explore.

"I want to be your wife," she whispered then reached up and brushed a kiss across his lips.

The moment their lips met, desire like she'd never imagined consumed her as his mouth covered hers hungrily. It was a glorious kiss and she wanted more. Her hands roamed over his broad shoulders, matching his urgency with her own unsated needs.

James was masculinity personified, a Corinthian oozing with confidence bordering on arrogance. His charming smile and far too handsome looks made women weak in the knees. His kisses could make a woman forget her virtues. He was without a doubt a rogue and a scoundrel and something else far too dangerous for her soul. And he was all hers.

He whispered, his breath hot against her ear, "I've wanted you like this for so long."

Evelina was shocked to admit it, but she had wanted him like this since she'd first spied him. "I want you."

James pulled back, surprise lining his features before a more intense emotion flooded his eyes. It was almost as if no one had ever said those words to him. But it was the truth. Evelina wanted him. Wanted him to make love to her. Wanted him to be her husband. Wanted him to be her partner in life.

James brushed kisses along her cheek, drifting softly toward her lips. "You taste like spring," he whispered before reclaiming her mouth in sweet seductive kisses that nearly took her breath away, sending tingles down her spine.

It was intoxicatingly delicious. She now understood how women succumbed to rakes.

He deepened the kiss, his tongue stroking, exploring. Evelina pressed closer, desperate to feel more of him as his hand moved under her dress to skim her hips and thighs.

Jolts of pleasure shot through her and she caught her breath. She'd never known her body was capable of such a response. "That . . . that is . . . divine. I want . . . more."

In the next moment, he swooped her up into his arms and started toward the door. She was about to question when he said, "I will not make love to you for the first time in my study. I want to take my time, savoring every inch of you."

Within moments they were in his suite. The warmth from the fire was no match for the inferno blazing between them. Their clothes practically melted off their bodies as heat and passion enveloped them.

Gently he eased her down onto the bed, then joined her. She drew his face down to hers and kissed him with a hunger that seemed to startle them both. It felt so right to be here with him, feeling the length of his muscular form against the smooth softness of hers.

Leaving her mouth burning with fire, his lips seared a path down her neck, across her chest, to her aching breasts. His lips brushed lightly, encircling each, before his tongue took one nipple in his mouth and he suckled.

Her whole body felt alight with all the sensations racing through her. She was shocked at her own eager response to the touch of his lips as she gave into pleasure. This intimacy with James was what she'd been longing, craving from the moment they'd met. It was so much more than two bodies coming together. It was two souls merging into one.

JAMES HAD NEVER wanted a woman the way he wanted Evelina. It was almost beyond comprehension, and so much more than sexual desire. No woman had ever felt so good, so perfect in his arms. He wanted to take his time, savor every inch of her, bring her pleasure. He suspected that he could make love to his wife all night and still want more.

What was happening to him? He made a point of never losing control and yet, whenever Evelina was near, he felt forever out of control.

Slowly he caressed the soft lines of her waist and hips with his hand. He took his time kissing her soft skin, inhaling her intoxicating scent, and memorizing every curve. Evelina was beyond responsive to his touch, encouraging him with soft moans of pleasure. He was desperate to feel her, to be inside her. Ever so gently, he slid into her, her muscles gripping him tighter, welcoming him into her body. She moaned his name and that was his undoing. In one thrust, he broke through her barrier.

"You're mine," she whispered.

*You're mine.* He'd never truly belonged to anyone, had never wanted to until this moment. It was almost too good to be true.

"I'm yours." He took her lips in a slow, thoughtful kiss, unable to express with words just what he was feeling in his heart.

Together they found a rhythm that bound their bodies in exquisite harmony, soaring higher until they found their mutual release. Contentment and peace flowed between them as James kept his wife within the folds of his arms as he drifted off to sleep.

A SOFT MOAN brushed across his chest as the scent of vanilla infiltrated his dreams, stirring desire anew. The world around him slowly came into focus. His lovely wife was still asleep, her long auburn locks flowing down her naked body.

James kissed the top of her head. He'd never spent an entire night with a woman, never woken up beside one. His whole adult life, he'd found lust, but he had never experienced such desire and passion. Until now.

This was . . . truly intimate.

For the first time in his life, James felt as if he was right where he was supposed to be. But lurking in the dark recesses of his mind, doubt began to rear its venomous head. Was this too good to be true?

# Chapter Fourteen

E VELINA HAD NEVER imagined married life could be this blissful. Their marriage may not be one of all-encompassing love, but over the past week, James had shown her time and again how much he cared. It wasn't in huge, grand gestures, but in dozens of little ones that he showed he'd been listening and cared. Everything from writing awful poetry, to sharing his thoughts, to keeping her safe within the fold of his arms each night. She truly hoped with time, he would begin to feel the same about her as she did about him.

The more time she spent with her husband, the more she fell in love with him. He may have been known throughout the *ton* as a rake, but she suspected that was just a façade to protect his heart, which was turning out to be quite sensitive. Oh, to be sure, he'd had his fair share of women over the years, but James had confided that he never shared anything of himself with them, never had wanted to until Evelina. She knew him not to be a man of many flowery words, but the tenderness in his eyes and sincerity in his voice had spoken volumes.

"Is my wife ready?" his deep voice called to her from the adjoining room, sending delicious ripples of pleasure down her back as remembrances of their lovemaking just a short time ago flooded her thoughts.

Evelina turned from her dressing table, her heart skipping a beat as she watched James enter her room wearing dark navy breeches and matching coat. How was it possible that he could continue to look even more handsome?

"I wish we could stay in tonight," she said in what she hoped was a seductive tone hinting at what she truly desired.

"And what would we do if we stayed in?" he said with an enticing half-smile, clearly understanding her meaning.

Heat engulfed her as thoughts of how they could fill the night infiltrated her being. "I'm sure we could think of something."

James strolled across the room and in the next moment, she was in his arms, being kissed—no, ravished—by her husband. She wrapped her arms about his neck, pressing her body closer to his, desperate to feel more of him.

Something intense flared between them before her husband pulled back slightly. "I think we had better save this for later, my sweetness," James said in a labored breath as he eased the kisses. "Jessica will not be pleased if she is late."

Normally Evelina would be the sound voice of reason, but her husband stirred a desire within that made all common sense flitter away. "Until later," she whispered as she nibbled his lips.

James rested his forehead against hers. "I will be counting the seconds until I can ravish you."

Feeling quite bold with the playful banter, she said, "Shall we get the evening started then? The sooner we leave—"

"The sooner I can have you in my bed." He trailed kisses across her cheek to her ear. "There are still so many pleasures I wish to teach you."

Oh dear, how would she ever focus on chaperoning Jessica this evening?

BY THE TIME they'd entered the ballroom, James was questioning his sanity. Evelina and Jessica were conversing with Lady Middleton—Evelina's beloved Aunt Imogene—who'd just returned from Bath, while he stood off to one side, trying to blend in to the wall. He never imagined that *he* would want to be a wallflower. For all of his life, he'd been out in the open for all to see, to gossip about, and now . . . he wanted nothing more than to retreat from Society with his wife.

Why on earth had he agreed to attend this evening?

*You wanted to be near to your wife.*

Even so, he found these events tedious, even more so since he'd married. Spending a night with Evelina in the quiet of their home, talking, playing billiards, and making love was now far more to his liking. Gone were the days when he'd stay out till the wee hours of the morning, searching for whatever could bring him some semblance of contentment, even for the briefest of moments. Now, he wanted to spend his days and nights with his wife. Evelina was more than just a woman to fill his bed. She'd become a friend and confidante. Someone he could truly be himself with.

"Oh, Lord Raine, I didn't expect to see you here this evening," Lady Spalding said as she greeted him.

"And whyever not?" He could barely keep the annoyance from his voice. He had no patience for gossipmongers, this one in particular. He suspected she had caused great harm with her callous words during her tenure within the *ton*. He was far too familiar with the gossip she'd spewed about him over the years.

"As if I have to explain why to you." Her words came at him all at once, in one rambling breath. "Still, your cousin seems to be quite in demand this Season. It's a good thing the gossip hasn't touched her, what with your sister's elopement, and then all the talk surrounding your wife's salon." She tsked several times, expressing disapproval. "And then there are the rumors surrounding Signorina Giordano."

*Salon?*

Since returning to Town, Evelina hadn't hosted a single one

to his knowledge. Had she been secretly hosting the gathering and keeping it from him? Doubt over the time they'd spent together started to creep into his thoughts once again. No, he would have certainly known if she were hosting those—

*Wait.*

Did Lady Spalding say Signorina Giordano?

"What are you—"

"Enjoy your evening, Lord Raine," Lady Spalding interrupted with a snicker, then walked away.

Oh, how he despised that woman *and* her insinuations.

James knew her words were nothing more than vile rumors. He'd done nothing wrong. None of this was true. He and Evelina had had a tumultuous beginning, but over the past weeks, things had changed. What he didn't know was who was creating the lies and for what purpose. None of it made sense to him.

James watched as Evelina offered him a seductive smile across the room before strolling away with her aunt and Jessica, leaving him festering in his own thoughts.

"You look like you want to kill someone," Lonsdale said as he approached, taking the spot against the wall beside James. His friend certainly had a way with words at the most inopportune times.

"Lady Spalding decided to enlighten me with tidbits of hearsay." It would be more accurate to say outrageous accusations founded on lies.

"I now understand the look. However, I do not believe she is the source."

James was of the same mindset, but he wanted to know why his friend thought so, too. "Why do you say that?"

"Lady Spalding and even Lady Shephard, are not conniving enough." Lonsdale caught James' look of disbelief and clarified. "Oh, don't get me wrong. The pair of them are quite disagreeable but are also most desperate to be accepted by those who they deem influential within the *ton*." He shook his head several times. "No, someone else is guiding those puppets' strings."

"I agree, and I intend to find out who." James needed to discover who was at the source of this tittle-tattle. "Let me know if you hear anything."

James didn't wait for his friend to respond but took his leave. He needed to clear his head and plot his next course of action. Easing his way through the crush, James headed for the terrace.

The cool evening air wisped past him, carrying away some of the troubled thoughts plaguing his mind, leaving only the most pressing to deal with. Why was his name constantly at the heart of this Season's worst rumors? Usually, the *ton* quickly moved from one scandal to the next, especially when there was no further fodder. And James had most certainly not given them anything.

"*Buonasera*, Lord Raine," the sultry voice of the renowned Italian actress drifted across the terrace.

"I am not interested in what you're offering, Signorina Giordano," he stated bluntly, meaning every word. He had no intention of wasting time letting the woman down gently. She wasn't the gentle sort. At least now he knew why Lady Spalding had mentioned her so particularly.

"You used to be," she murmured as she strolled toward him, hips swaying in a way that was meant to entice, but had the exact opposite effect on him.

"That was a long time ago." James had no interest in opera singers or actresses—that was in the past. The only woman who heated his blood and stirred his desire was Evelina, and he was about to say as much when Signorina Giordano interrupted.

"*Non molto tempo fa*, not so long ago," she said as she snaked a single finger down his arm.

James backed away as he ground out, "I do not know what you are up to, but—"

A loud gasp rent his words, slashing through the protest forming on his lips. "And I thought you were devoted to your wife," Lady Jerome said before quickly turning and dashing back inside the ballroom with Lady Spalding on her heels.

Without thought he followed the mischief-maker into the ballroom, but the woman had struck faster than lightning on a stormy night, her words piercing through the ballroom with intensity and force. Within a matter of seconds, tittle-tattle surrounded him, threatening to consume and destroy.

James had done nothing wrong, and yet all eyes centered on him as if he'd just committed the crime of the century.

*I need to find Evelina and explain before . . .*

He spied his wife a dozen feet away, his cousin standing beside her. Her green eyes full with hurt and humiliation. He would not further agitate the situation, but remove them all immediately.

"Shall we take our leave?" he said as he approached Evelina and Jessica.

"I think that would be for the best," his wife said. She held her chin high and walked out of the ballroom as if nothing untoward had happened, as if Lady Jerome had not just informed half the *ton* that James was on the veranda with Signorina Giordano, as if she wasn't affected by the vicious gossiping tongues.

The carriage ride passed in silence. They walked up the stairs in silence. And silence continued to envelope them as they stood face to face in their suite of rooms.

"Nothing happened," he confessed in earnest, desperate for her to believe him. "I informed her that I wasn't interested in anything she was offering. We exchanged words. That was all."

Evelina stared at him, as if assessing whether he was telling the truth.

"Is she your mistress?" Her voice was thick with sorrow.

"No." He had never lied to her before and he would not start now, and he would not keep his past from her. But how could he put this delicately? "But . . . before you and I met . . ." He ran a trembling hand through his hair. He stood on the precipice of happiness, and one wrong move could send him spiraling into a dark abyss. "I want you to know the truth." Evelina nodded her head slowly. "Several years ago, we were intimate on occasion, but it didn't mean anything." Desperation for her to believe him permeated his words. "She never meant anything to me."

Evelina looked into his eyes and held his gaze for several long, painful, silent seconds before speaking. "I believe you." Although her face was lined with hurt, her words were firm.

The tension in his shoulders eased. How could he help his wife to understand? "I would never do anything to hurt you."

"Thank you," she said as she offered him a sad sort of smile, then retired to her room.

James did not know how to prove his words, his dedication, but he would find a way.

DAYS HAD PASSED since the incident with Signorina Giordano, and, although Evelina believed James, she could not shake the nagging feeling that something awful was lurking on the horizon, waiting to destroy the fragile happiness they'd discovered.

The sorrow she felt was almost too much to bear. She needed to talk to someone about all the thoughts and emotions she couldn't put into words. Perhaps Aunt Imogene could offer some words of comfort.

Evelina glanced at the clock. *Half past two. Perfect.* She had just enough time to visit her aunt for a couple of hours before she needed to return home and ready for Lady Ingram's dinner party.

Before long, Evelina was walking up the front steps to Aunt Imogene's London home. Fond memories of time spent with her sisters here last Season flooded her thoughts. So much had changed, and in such a short span of time. Oh, how she missed them. Perhaps once the Season was over, she could visit them.

"Good afternoon, Lady Raine," Roger said as he opened the door. "I informed Lady Middleton of your—"

"Evelina!" her aunt's joyful voice echoed down the stairs. "I wasn't expecting a visit from you today."

As Aunt Imogene descended the last step, Evelina rushed into her embrace. Emotion choked her words. "I just wanted to see you."

Her aunt pulled back and assessed her for a moment. "We won't be disturbed in the parlor." Taking Evelina's hand in her own, she guided her toward the bright cheery room that always seemed to make her feel better.

"What is bothering you, dearest?" Aunt Imogene said as they took a seat side by side on the damask sofa.

Evelina did not know where to begin. It wasn't as if anything was precisely the matter, just more a feeling of trouble looming. "I don't know," she confessed in a sheepish tone. Perhaps she was being nonsensical.

"Does it have something to do with gossip?" Aunt Imogene said with a sideways glance.

The words that Evelina had been holding at bay began to pour from her mouth. "It seems that every gossip sheet contains a new sordid tale about James' misdeeds or mine. James constantly denies the tittle-tattle, and I believe him—certainly the gossip about me is untrue—but why won't it end? It constantly wears on us. Surely, we are not that interesting. I don't understand why the *ton* won't just let us be. And what about Jessica? She is such a sweet girl. Her chances for a good match should not be marred by all this—"

"Take a breath, dearest." And if to emphasize her point, Aunt Imogene took in a deep breath and exhaled slowly. "Better." She offered a smile. "From what I've heard, Jessica has many prospects. I don't think the gossip has ruined her. I truly don't know why the gossipmongers find Lord Raine so fascinating. He certainly has not done anything untoward from what I've heard from any reliable people. There have been far more scandalous goings on this Season. What does your heart tell you?"

Evelina worried her hands as she searched her heart. James had never given her cause to doubt his words. He'd been most sincere toward her, sharing parts of himself he'd never shared with anyone, and had been honest with her about his past. He'd professed that the women of his past were just that, in his past, and those liaisons meant nothing to him now. And his actions bore that out. Her heart calmed.

"To trust him."

"Then do just that. It may not be easy at times, but I think he cares about you more than he is willing to admit."

Her aunt's words gave her hope. "You truly think so?"

Aunt Imogene nodded her head. "Yes. He may just not know how to express it yet. His family is not like ours. It may take time."

Evelina's cheeks heated with the thought of all the intimacies they'd shared already. He certainly knew how to express desire and passion. But that wasn't love. Why were matters of the heart so complicated?

"Thank you, Aunt Imogene. I always enjoy our talks."

"Anytime, dearest." Evelina melted into her aunt's hug. Oh, how she missed spending time with her family.

They'd spent the remainder of the afternoon catching up on, well . . . everything. Aunt Imogene shared stories of her time in Bath and visiting friends, while Evelina shared her ideas on the improvements she was considering for Raine Hall. It was a most enjoyable time.

When the clock chimed five times, Evelina looked up at it in surprise. Where had the afternoon gone?

"Are you going to Lady Ingram's tonight?" Evelina asked, hoping to spend a little more time with her relative this evening.

"No, I'm going Lady Kirkland's musicale this evening."

"I hope Lord Kirkland doesn't disappoint his mother again."

Aunt Imogene rolled her eyes. "That is quite the hope, but I do hope for my friend's sake, that he does not. Enjoy your evening, dearest."

A short time later, feeling much lighter and more like herself, Evelina was in her suite and readying for Lady Ingram's dinner party. Although James had not returned from his business, he did leave a note. She opened the letter and read the rather awful poem he'd written.

*My Sweetness,*

*I have been delayed, but don't let that sway. I will meet you and Jessica at Lady Ingram's. I will not stray.*

*When midnight comes, you will hear the drum, our passion ignites. Until then, think of me.*

*James*

Evelina giggled with his words. James may not be a great poet, but his effort with the written word did bring a smile to her face.

# Chapter Fifteen

E VELINA PACED THE length of the study. Where was James? He hadn't gone to Lady Ingram's dinner party, leaving her to make excuses for his absence. Worse still, those in attendance had come to their own conclusion, namely that James was visiting one of his many paramours. Without fail, every time Evelina and James had found even the slightest bit of peace, another piece of gossip emerged. The whispers had flurried around her through the entire dinner party.

Although James had constantly reassured her, doubt was always rearing its pesky head. How could it not when his name was constantly being circulated? One would think after all these months, the rumormongers could have found a different source of entertainment.

Perhaps she shouldn't confront him, and just trust him. *I do trust him.* But she also deserved at the very least to know why he hadn't joined them tonight when they'd expected him.

She continued to pace back and forth, pondering what she should do, when James strolled into the room, none the wiser about all that she'd endured this evening at the hands of the gossips.

"Where have you been?" the angry, accusatory words rushed from her mouth without censorship. She hadn't meant to be so harsh, but her nerves were frayed.

"I had business to tend to and by the time it concluded it was too late—"

"You missed Lady Ingram's dinner party, and I had little to offer in terms of excuses." She folded her arms and attempted to keep her temper in check, but it had been at a boiling point all evening and in the next breath the misery finally broke through her fragile control. "Dammit, James. Do you have any idea what the gossips are saying? How much louder they get when you're not there?"

"I would never do anything to cause you harm," he said with a sincerity that, while obvious, did little to ease Evelina's angst. "They're just rumors. I would never—"

"Then why is *your* name, and no other gentlemen, constantly linked to all these exceptionally beautiful women this Season?"

He took a cautious step closer. "I don't know. I—"

"I'm tired of the gossip, the whispers at every function and . . ." And she felt deflated, as if a thousand horses had trampled across her heart. She bit back tears of grief.

"What would you have me do?" His words were filled with all the frustration she too was feeling.

She didn't know. What could he do? What could she do? They'd tried to present themselves as a happily married couple, rising above the gossip—and perhaps for a brief time they were, and did—but that only seemed to incur more rumors. All the whispers and words were destroying them and their happiness.

Evelina was exhausted. She should have never agreed to this bargain, to any of it. She should have found a different course rather than marrying a notorious rake, but now it was too late. And then she'd done the one thing she absolutely shouldn't have: fallen in love with her husband.

Piercing pain like she'd never before experienced shot through her heart. What was going to happen to them?

The silence continued to linger, neither having any answers.

James shook his head. "I see. I will leave you alone," he said, his voice resigned, tired, almost hopeless. And without further argument, he walked out of the room, walked away from her.

Evelina stood, staring at the open door, hoping, praying he would return, but minutes ticked by in slow measure, and he still did not return to her.

She should never have let her temper get the better of her. Weighed down with regret and sorrow, she trudged to her room, hoping to find at least a little solace from the terrible ache ripping through her insides.

LONG TEMPESTUOUS HOURS later, Evelina stretched her aching limbs. She'd barely slept, spending most of the night tossing and turning and missing James. She detested how they ended things last night, that he had not come to her bed.

She didn't want to fight and argue with him or even to exchange unkind words. She wanted to believe the kind, passionate words he spoke, to believe the truly awful poetry he wrote about desire and passion, but most of all, she wanted to believe in the two of them, in their connection to each other.

Evelina went to the window and gazed across the sleeping garden. The sun was just starting to make its presence known to the world, ready to declare its intentions of warmth, light, and new promises. She wished she could declare her intentions to her husband as easily.

*You can.*

It was as if the clouds parted, revealing her heart's true desire. *I've never told James how I felt, how I love him.*

There were so many things she'd wanted to say, but she'd never found the words, or truth be told, the confidence. She was just as stubborn as he, and she knew her instinct was to draw back, but she wanted to make things right with him. She wanted to break away from the past and old habits and start anew.

Perhaps Aunt Imogene could take over chaperoning duties for Jessica for the remainder of the Season, and Evelina and James could escape to the country, just the two of them.

She went straight for the door that joined their rooms. This was the start of a new day for her, for them. She would tell him that she believed him, not the rumors, and declare her love for him.

*But what if he didn't feel the same?*

He desired her, that much she knew. But was it enough? Would he welcome her declaration or see it is a nuisance?

*You'll never know how he feels if you don't act first. Be brave.*

She sucked in her breath, opened the door, and charged into his room like a knight out to slay a dragon.

The drapes had been partially pulled, allowing hazy morning sunlight to drift into the warm space. A hint of jasmine hung in the air.

*Jasmine?*

Evelina stopped and stared at the large bed. Her husband's bare chest rose and fell in gentle slumber, but next to him . . .

Long blonde waves flowed over the side of the bed. Hurt and betrayal rose up like bile in her throat, strangling her dreams. *No. He didn't . . . was this his mistress . . . he said he never . . .*

The rumors *were* true. She edged closer, not wanting to confirm her suspicions but needing to know. A soft feminine moan emanated from under the covers.

*How could he?* Her mind screamed as tears fell like rain, pouring down her cheeks.

Evelina could not stay, would not stay. Everything she'd begun to believe about them, their future, had been a lie.

Wiping away the tears with a rough hand, she retreated to her room, closed the door with quiet caution, and then locked the adjoining door. There would be time enough to scream, to feel. But now . . . she just needed to leave.

JAMES OPENED HIS eyes just a sliver, but the pounding in his head forced them closed again.

*What the bloody hell happened last night?* The last thing he remembered was having a drink after that difficult conversation with Evelina.

He rubbed his aching temples as he attempted to open his eyes once again. Sliver by sliver, he forced his eyelids up. Bright sunlight streaked into the room from the partially opened drape.

*What time was it?*

He stretched his sore limbs, pushing the covers off his naked torso. A gentle whisp of jasmine rose up from the warm bed.

*Jasmine? Evelina never wore that scent. She detested that smell.*

Alarm bells rang through his mind as he ripped the remaining covers from the bed. He stared down at a very naked, petite, blonde-haired woman.

*What the hell was going on?*

The woman began to pull at the covers as she voiced her displeasure at his actions. "Why did you—"

"Who the hell are you?" he demanded.

Her voice turned from annoyed to silky in a single breath. "Certainly, you could not forget me that quickly Lord Raine?" She reached out as if to touch him, but he jumped out of the bed and strode across the room to put his clothes on. "Why so shy, my lord? After what happened—"

"Nothing happened."

"Are you certain, my lord?" her tone dropped suggestively.

*Had something happened?*

*No.* In all his wild years, he had never brought a mistress to his family home, never even spent the entire night with one. Plus, he had made a promise to . . .

*Evelina.*

He stormed across the room, ignoring the sultry words of the woman in his bed, to the door that joined their suites.

Locked.

He pounded on the door with a firm fist. "Evelina!" A slight crack creaked in the wood door as his fist hit the panel. When he received no response, he pounded once more, his mind racing. "Dammit, open up!"

"Pardon me, my lord," his valet said as he entered the room from the main door. If he was shocked to see the stranger in his bed, he did not let on. "Lady Raine went for an early morning ride and—"

"When will she return?"

"She is due to return at any time. She's been gone nearly two hours and—"

"I want to be informed the moment she returns. Have my bath readied, and get that . . . that woman out my house," he demanded as he pointed to the blonde reclining casually in his bed as if nothing untoward had happened. "And bring me something for the ache in my head!" He hadn't meant to sound so curt, but he was still trying to sort out what had happened.

His temper was dangling by a thread. What was he going to tell Evelina when she returned? *The truth.* Would she believe the truth? That he had not a clue as to who the woman was or why she was in his bed.

Over an hour later, the pounding in his head had eased to a dull ache, he was slightly refreshed from his bath, and the mattress that *that* woman had been on had been removed. He then went downstairs to discover if his wife had returned from her morning ride, though he still hadn't quite worked out what he was going to say.

But no sooner had he descended the last step than his mother approached. He inhaled deeply, inwardly shook his head, and said a silent prayer. *Give me strength.*

"What are you doing here?"

"Clearly, you've forgotten. Your sister and her children are due to arrive, and since Henrietta insisted on staying with you rather than at my home, I—"

"My lord," Martin said as he rushed in, his features flushed "the lad who accompanied Lady Raine on her morning ride just returned. Your wife has gone missing."

James felt as if all his happiness had been ripped out from beneath him this morning. He tried to maintain his calm. Losing his temper would not get him the answers he needed.

"What to do you mean *missing?*"

"They were out on their ride and got separated. He searched for her, but after nearly an hour, the stableboy decided to return for reinforcements."

Damn, what could have happened to her? She had to be safe. "Bring the lad to me and send a search party to find my wife."

And with that command, Martin left.

James turned his attention to his mother. "Did you happen to see Evelina this morning?"

"My dear boy, you know very well that we avoid each other at all costs in order to keep the peace," she said with a dismissive air. "Now, if you will excuse me, I have much to arrange before my grandchildren arrive."

His mother's tone and attitude did not sit well with him. She'd never given much thought to her grandchildren before. In fact, she'd always insisted they remain in the nursery, out of sight. That was why Henrietta and her family always stayed with James when in Town. This was another item to deal with later. First things first. He needed to discover what had happened to his wife, then confess . . . what exactly?

*Nothing happened,* he tried to convince himself. *But what if something had?*

By the time he reached his study, his mood had darkened into an unfathomable abyss. He slumped into his chair, as he attempted to sort through the ramblings in his foggy brain.

"My lord," a young stableboy nervously began as he entered the room, "you wanted to see me?"

"I need you to tell me in precise detail all the events of this morning."

The lad twisted his cap in his hands as he began to recount the morning. "Lady Raine came to the stables and requested Hermes to be saddled and—"

"She requested *my* horse?"

Hermes was the fastest horse in his possession. He knew her to be an experienced rider but why would she . . .

For the second time that morning, alarm bells resounded in his head. Had she discovered what happened, the woman inexplicably in his bed?

"Yes, my lord. All was well until she kicked the horse into a gallop and took off. I tried to keep up, but that horse was too fast . . ." His words died and his features contorted as if waiting for James to unleash his fury upon him.

It wasn't the lad's fault. His gut told him Evelina had discovered his liaison, or possible liaison. *Damn.*

James would scour all of London until she was found.

# Chapter Sixteen

E VELINA WAS LIVID, hurt, and completely destroyed by James' infidelity. She knew she had to leave, but she did not have the means to accomplish such a feat on her own. This was precisely one of the traps the Grace sisters had warned against at their salon, and Evelina had walked right into it.

After donning her riding habit, she went to the stables. She knew one of the grooms would be assigned to accompany her, but once in the park, she planned to unleash Hermes' strength and leave the groom behind none the wiser as to where she was headed. It was a simple plan, though it was fraught with the possibility of all sorts of problems. But she could not think about those. All she could focus on was leaving, leaving London, leaving the gossip, leaving James. If she thought about anything else, including why she was leaving, she might break down and cry. Again.

They'd just entered the park when the opportunity she needed presented itself.

"It is a nice morning," the stableboy said as he inhaled the crisp morning air, taking in his surroundings.

With the lad looking in the opposite direction, Evelina kicked Hermes into a full gallop, encouraging the horse to unleash his full strength. The powerful horse was no match for the mare the stableboy was riding. Less than fifteen minutes later, Evelina had successfully outmaneuvered him and was making straight for Aunt Imogene's home.

She wasn't prepared to answer a barrage of questions, or any questions really, and hoped that her aunt wouldn't press.

Within moments upon entering the house, she was greeted by her aunt. "Good morning, Evelina. It's quite early—"

"I need your help, Aunt Imogene."

Somehow Evelina managed to relay a very condensed version of what had happened without crying. And much to her relief, instead of questions, Aunt Imogene offered her carriage and one of the downstairs maids to join her on her escape.

Once everything was arranged, all Evelina had to do was wait for the carriage to be readied, and then she would be on her way to Grimsby Hall. She was most desperate to see at least one sister, and Theodora lived a day and a half's journey from Town. Once there, she could think about the next step.

"All is ready, Lady Middleton," Roger offered, then took his leave, giving them a moment to say goodbye.

"Are you certain you want to leave—"

"I have to, Aunt Imogene. I . . ."

"No need to explain, dearest." Aunt Imogene brought her within the folds of a warm embrace. "You needn't worry about anything. Hermes will be returned to Lord Raine in due course. And don't fret over Jessica. I'll see that she finishes the Season with a marriage proposal from Mr. Drinkwater."

It was no surprise that the two had formed a *tendre*. Mr. Drinkwater was all that Jessica talked about every waking moment. Even James had taken notice and did not object to the match. And just yesterday, Aunt Imogene had informed Evelina that she had it on good authority that the gentleman intended to ask for Jessica's hand before the week was over. It was most promising.

"Thank you, Aunt Imogene."

MANY HOURS AND a horribly restless night spent at a traveling inn later, the carriage was finally turning down the long, familiar drive to Grimsby Hall. It was just as she remembered it with several wide, tree-lined avenues that branched off the main drive. Many pleasant days had been spent here with Theodora, and she hoped to regain some of that tranquility.

Her mind, body, and soul were completely exhausted. Since she'd discovered the truth about *his* infidelities, she had not allowed her mind to reflect. Soon she would be with Theodora, and then . . .

*I don't know.*

Hot tears stung the corners of her eyes. *Don't think about him,* she demanded. Just get inside the house, then you can cry.

Several minutes later, the conveyance stopped in front of the impressive four-story manor. The numerous windows glistened in the sunlight.

No sooner had Evelina alighted, than she heard Theodora's excited squeal, followed by Luna's excited *woof.* "Evelina! I didn't know we'd be expecting you!"

With just the sound of her name in her sister's voice, Evelina burst into tears. Loud sobs shook through her. She felt her sister's warm embrace, guiding her into the house but didn't notice anything of her surroundings as tears blurred her vision. A short time later, the two sisters were alone in the drawing room.

Theodora offered another handkerchief, then smoothed the wet locks off Evelina's face. "Are you ready to tell me what happened?"

She'd written to both her sisters frequently over the past months but had never confessed the truth about the gossip that was constantly being spread through Town, or of her changing feelings for James, or of so many of the things that had happened.

She took a deep breath, hoping to steady her voice so she

could relay her story. "We didn't marry for love . . ." *Love.* As she said the word, the tears that she was desperately trying to keep at bay threatened to unleash their fury once again. She sniffled several times, attempting to regain her composure. *She'd fallen in love with him.* "And now . . . now it's too late. He promised to remain faithful . . ." The moment the last word crossed her trembling lips, the deluge began again.

Theodora just held her, held her and offered soft words of comfort. But how did one ever find comfort when their heart was shattering?

Several minutes, perhaps more—Evelina truly did not know—passed before there was a knock on the door. Her brother-in-law peered in, motioning for Theodora.

"I'll be right back," Theodora said as she kissed Evelina's temple.

"I don't know what happened," she heard her sister explain to Damian. "She won't stop crying."

Other words were exchanged before her sister returned to her side and simply continued to hold her. She wanted to talk, even thought it might make her feel better, but there were simply no words for what Evelina was feeling. At that moment, all she wanted was for the pain to go away, all she wanted was to go numb.

Theodora didn't try to ask any more questions until Evelina stopped crying.

"Are you ready to tell me what happened?" Theodora finally asked as she rubbed her hand in soothing circles across Evelina's back.

She nodded her head, then took a deep breath to steady her nerves, hoping this time it would actually help. "There was a woman in *his* bed." The betrayal burned her throat with each word she spoke, and the pain in her heart magnified. How would she ever survive this?

Theodora's brows creased together in confusion. Evelina couldn't blame her sister for being bewildered, but it was tiresome just the same. Couldn't she just read Evelina's thoughts? Then she wouldn't have to recount any of it and be spared the pain of reliving it.

But luck was not on Evelina's side.

"Perhaps it would be best if you started from the beginning," Theodora suggested as she took Evelina's hand and gave a slight squeeze of encouragement.

Despite her bitter embarrassment over all that had happened, Evelina rambled on and on, telling her sister the truth about how they came to be husband and wife, how Harold had treated her upon hearing of the scandal, how she kept the truth from her and Alexandra, how *his* name was now constantly on the wagging tongues of gossipmongers, how over the past months she'd fallen in love with her husband, and how she'd been wrong to believe he might care for her in return. Their love was not the everlasting love most girls dreamed about but a temporary one where love soured under the weight of lies.

"Why didn't you tell us?" Theodora scolded in a loving way that only a dearest sister could. "We could have come to London and aided you."

The reasons she'd kept things from her siblings seemed so childish now, although there were a couple of valid concerns. "Well . . . with Alexandra *enceinte* and you so recently married to Lord Grimsby, and—"

"And you're my sister." She brought Evelina into a sisterly embrace and held her tightly. "Never keep secrets from us. We're on this journey together. And I know without a doubt that Alexandra feels the same," she said in a tone so sincere that Evelina's tears threatened to begin anew, not from sorrow, but from the joy of having family who cared so deeply. Her words turned solemn, "Do you really believe Lord . . ."

Evelina shook her head fervently, silently begging her sister not to say *his* name.

"I understand. We're back to that, are we?" Theodora shook her head. "Very well, do you really believe that *he* doesn't care?"

"I don't know. I just feel so . . . so . . ." She released a heavy sigh. "So lost."

*Knock. Knock. Knock.*

"Come in," her sister said.

Damian, Lord Grimsby, the reclusive earl that so many feared but who had a heart of gold, entered the room, and spoke to his wife. "All is ready for an early departure. I've sent word ahead of our pending arrival."

Evelina had been selfish. She hadn't even considered that her sister and brother-in-law may have had plans. Hopefully she could stay at Grimsby Hall and convalesce while they were gone. "Where are you—"

Damian stopped her with a kind look, and when he spoke his tone was most sincere. "Not Theodora and I, but we—all three of us—are traveling to see Alexandra and Niall at Blackburn Hall first thing in the morning."

She looked to her sister, then back to Damian. "You're taking me and Theodora to see Alexandra?"

"Family is what matters. It has been far too long since the three of you have been together." His words touched her heart more than she could ever express.

So consumed with grief, Evelina had only just then realized Damian was no longer hiding behind a half-mask, as he had for so many years. Several slightly raised ridges nearly the same color as the rest of the skin, streaked the right side of his face. But they weren't frightening in the least. She was glad he no longer feared showing the world who he was. The scars that had kept him hidden in shadows were no match for the truly exceptional man that he was.

"Thank you, Damian, for everything."

"You're most welcome, Evelina."

THE NEXT MORNING, the trio left Grimsby Hall. It was a trouble-free journey, but with each mile they traveled, the heartache that weighed Evelina down only intensified. Two days passed before they finally arrived at their sister's home.

Although Blackburn Hall bordered their childhood home, Charis Hall, the girls had never really spent any time there, despite being good friends with Niall and his younger sister, Naomi. Niall's mother had made certain the Grace sisters—all of the Grace family, really—were not welcome in *her* home. In the simplest terms, the Dowager Duchess of Blackburn was not a very nice person.

No sooner had the carriage stopped, than Alexandra was rushing down the front steps—far too quickly for someone in her condition—to greet them. Soon, the three Grace sisters were entangled in a loving embrace.

"Come inside and tell me all that has happened," Alexandra said she released them, then rubbed her large, extended stomach.

A short time later, the three sisters were ensconced in Alexandra's private parlor, a glowing fire chasing away the chill of the early evening. Evelina recounted all the events that had brought her to her sister's door. Although her heart still ached, Evelina's soul was a little more at peace now that she was with her sisters.

"It seems there was quite a bit going on in Town this Season," Alexandra said. That was an understatement if there ever was one. "Although I daresay, I am much happier here." The glow in her cheeks and softness in her eyes was most becoming on the expectant mother.

Evelina felt the pain sweeping inside her knowing she was now unlikely to experience the joy of motherhood with *him*.

"I think we're all happier being away from Society," Theodora chimed in.

Both her sisters were so content and in love. And she couldn't be more pleased for them. But what did the future hold for Evelina?

The whisper broke from her lips on a quiver. "What am I to

do?"

Alexandra kissed Evelina's cheek, then said, "I don't know, but we will think of something—"

"Together," Theodora finished Alexandra's sentence.

No matter what the future held, at the very least Evelina had a loving family, and that gave her great comfort.

# Chapter Seventeen

James had scoured Town, but there was no sign of Evelina or Hermes. Where had she gone? What had happened to her? He couldn't sleep. He could barely eat. Then, two days later his horse was delivered along with a note from Lady Middleton explaining that Evelina had left Town and required distance, and his world became much bleaker. Alcohol had become a constant companion, aiding James in his descent into oblivion. The world around him continued to live and thrive as James succumbed to his own personal hell.

Now he was certain—Evelina knew the truth of his infidelity and had left him. He had no one to blame but himself. He only wished he could remember that fateful night that destroyed the only happiness he'd ever truly known.

"It's been nearly a week. You must stop this!" his eldest sister declared as she stormed into his study, then slammed the door shut. "Sitting here wallowing in alcohol and despair is not going to help bring Evelina back."

He didn't bother to sit up but turned his head on the desk so he could look at her with one bleary eye. "You don't know what I did," the words tore from his mouth in agony.

"Do *you*?" Henrietta stood there with her hands on her hips, glaring down at him. Henrietta was ten years his senior and, in many ways, more of a mother to him than his own mother had ever been. "Your valet told me that you don't remember what happened, that you—"

"I woke up with a woman in my bed, a woman who was not my wife, and—"

"For all the years I've known you, you have never—not once—brought a woman other than your wife into this house or into any of your houses." She moved toward him and placed a gentle hand on his back. "It doesn't make sense. There must be some other explanation." When James didn't move, she kneeled down beside him. "We may not always have been close, but I know you. I know your character. I don't believe for one moment that you dishonored your vows."

He sat up, but slumped in his chair and shifted his gaze to her. "You don't?"

"No, I do not. Since the moment you met Evelina, there has been something different about you. Do you want to know what I think?"

He wanted to know and didn't want to know in equal measure. But in the end, curiosity won. He braced himself for some awful truth she was about to reveal as he nodded his head.

"I think you've been in love with Evelina since the very moment you met her. I think you went to the country house party not because of Daisy, but because you wanted to ensure that Evelina did not set her cap at another. I think you kissed her at Lady Holland's ball because you knew she would not disgrace her family and refuse to marry you."

"You seem to think a lot." It was a weak attempt at lightening the mood with a bit of deflection, but it was the best he could do at the moment.

"*And . . .*" James cringed slightly at his sister's forceful use of the three-letter word, but then Henrietta's tone softened. "I think you're scared to death to admit just how much you need her."

The words pierced his heart. Henrietta was right. He was terrified that one woman could consume him so. From the moment he'd met Evelina, all he could think about was her. All he wanted to plan for was Evelina. And now . . .

"What am I to do?"

"Discover the truth," Henrietta said, then waved her hand in front of her nose. "But first, you desperately need a bath. You reek of alcohol."

A COUPLE OF hours later and feeling much more like himself, James and his sister were plotting their next course of action.

What James had told Evelina the night of Lady Ingram's dinner party about tending to business was true. For weeks, he'd been trying to discover the source of the gossip, but to no avail. That night, he'd thought he had a breakthrough, but it turned out to be a false lead. Whoever was the source of all these rumors about James and Evelina had covered their tracks very well or—a more likely scenario—paid someone handsomely to keep their mouth shut.

James and Henrietta's plan for the day included Henrietta speaking with Lady Archibald while James was to figure out exactly who the woman in his bed was. He wasn't sure who had the more monumental task.

Hours later, James trudged up the steps to his house, beyond exhausted—both mentally and physically. Neither he nor Henrietta had had much luck in their respective tasks. For once in Lady Archibald's life, she had kept rather silent on the gossip surrounding James.

"May I have a word in private, my lord?" Martin said as he greeted James in the entry. He didn't really have the patience for household issues at the moment and was about to say as much when the trusted butler lowered his voice to a mere whisper. "It's in regard to Lady Raine."

*Evelina.*

Without wasting another moment, James went to his study with Martin following closely behind. It wasn't like his butler to be so secretive.

*It must be bad news.*

As soon as the door was closed, the words rushed from James' mouth. "My wife has been found?" He held his breath, praying his wife had not met with an unfortunate accident. He didn't know what he would do . . .

*No, Evelina was all right.* She had to be.

"No, my lord. There has been no word from or about Lady Raine, but I believe your mother may know something."

"My mother?" She never had cared for Evelina and made that known to anyone who would listen, and even to those who didn't want to listen. Remembrances of past arguments with her filled his mind. Would his mother purposefully harm his wife because of dislike?

"While you were out, your mother came, wanting to speak with you. While she was here, a letter was delivered bearing the seal of the Duke of Blackburn." Martin paused for a moment, as if to let the information he'd just relayed penetrate. "Lady Raine insisted on taking the letter and said she would deliver it to you."

He fought to keep his focus through his building rage. "Where is she now?"

"She left shortly after the letter arrived."

"Damn." He ran a frustrated hand through his hair. "Inform my sister that I have gone to pay a visit to our mother."

James stormed from his house with all the fury of a tornado breaking upon the land. His mother's residence was not far, and by the time he'd arrived, his rage had only gained momentum.

"Good afternoon—"

"Save the pleasantries, Jared," he began as he brushed past the butler. "Where is my mother?"

"She's readying for the evening, my lord" his voice quavered with each word he spoke. Clearly, his mother ruled her house with an iron fist. "May I send word that you are here?"

"I will see myself to her room." Under normal circumstances, James would not intrude on her personal space. But this was far from normal, and he preferred to catch her unawares.

He took the stairs two at a time, too anxious to discover what was in the letter from the Duke of Blackburn to tarry. He didn't bother knocking as he burst into her room.

"James," his mother gasped as she clasped a hand to her heaving chest. "You startled me. Is anything the matter?" Although her tone was sweet on the surface, there was a note of bitterness underneath.

"You tell me." He stood his ground and just watched, waited.

Seconds ticked by and she did not respond, but James knew this game of hers all too well. He would not back down. He would watch her every movement. Sooner or later, she would reveal something.

Her eyes shifted ever so slightly from him to the side table across the room. He quickly glanced that way and spied her reticule on the table. In an instant, he was across the room and emptying the contents.

"How dare you go through my things and . . ." Her words died off as he held the letter that had been in the reticule.

"How dare *you* take from me," his words were slow, deep, harsh. Her eyes widened, but she did not speak. James opened the missive and read the contents to himself.

He drew in a deep breath through his nose and then let out a long sigh of relief. Evelina was with her sisters. She was safe.

With that knowledge, James was able to turn his full attention on his mother. He suspected she knew far more about this entire situation than she was letting on, and he wouldn't leave until he got all his answers.

The prolonged silence must have been eating away at her conscience. In a voice that was uncharacteristically uneasy, she finally asked, "What news from Blackburn?"

Before he could decide how to expose this bluff, her lady's maid knocked, then entered the room, in an almost fearful panic.

"Pardon me, Lady Raine," the timid maid began before she began to ramble. "Jared told her to go away but *that* woman insists on seeing you and won't leave until she speaks with you. She is creating quite the scene downstairs and—"

James narrowed his gaze, watching his mother closely, assessing. "What woman?" He enunciated the words slowly, with firmness.

"I . . ." She swallowed nervously. "I . . . don't know who it may be."

Without a doubt, she was lying.

James did not waste another moment, but rushed from the room and down the stairs, following the sounds of an irate female voice that was echoing from the front of the house, while ignoring the other irate female screaming after him.

He stopped short when he saw an attractive blonde-haired woman giving Jared more than an earful.

*The woman from his bed.*

"Do not believe a word she says," his mother commanded while taking in gasps of air, out of breath from chasing after him.

James waved a hand to silence her, then turned to the blonde-haired woman. "Who are you and why are you here?"

She pointed a trembling finger at his mother. "I want no part in her schemes any longer. I have to think of my future and that of my . . ." Her words trailed off in desperation, leaving James to wonder what sort of bargain his mother had made.

"What were you promised?"

His mother stepped forward. There was panic in her voice when she spoke. "Don't believe anything a . . . a . . . a common strumpet—"

James turned a harsh glare on his mother. "Not another word from you." He softened his tone and addressed the stranger once again. If his suspicions were correct, she was a victim of his mother's schemes as much as he. "Why don't we start with your name?"

"Louisa. Louisa Proust."

He nodded his head in greeting. "Now, Miss Proust, how exactly did you end up in my bed?"

She worried her hands, and her voice trembled. "I . . . that is . . ." She shook her head several times before continuing. "I . . . I am not proud of how I earn money but . . . I have a son to care for." Her face brightened as she spoke about her child. "He's such a darling little boy. Oh, and so intelligent."

His patience was hanging by a thread, yet somehow, he remained calm. "But how did you come to be in *my* bed?"

"*She* came to me and offered a lot of money if I would spend the night with you." Her voice was low, as if she were unsure whether she should be speaking about a lady when she was still in the room.

Thinking back on that night, the only thing he remembered after speaking with Evelina was taking a glass of brandy. He could not recall another single detail from that night. He needed to know exactly what had happened between him and Miss Proust. "And then what?"

She lowered her voice further and nodded toward his mother, "Well . . . *she* snuck me into your room—"

His mother began to protest vehemently, "I would never do any such—"

"Jared, please escort my mother to her parlor. Do *not* let her leave. I will deal with her shortly."

"Yes, my lord."

Much to James' surprise, his mother did not put up an argument, but went quietly with the butler.

Now that one distraction was removed, he could focus on Miss Proust. "Please continue."

She swallowed hard, then recounted the evening. "You were already asleep in the bed and snoring when I entered."

"So, we didn't . . ." He *had* been faithful to his wife.

"No, my lord. We slept, and nothing more." She placed her hand over her heart, then added, "I promise. Nothing else happened."

He fought the urge to leave immediately to go to Evelina. First, he needed all the answers to his questions. "And why are you here now?"

Tears of shame slid down her cheeks. "I want no more of her schemes. I want my money and that's all."

"And what was her scheme?"

"She said all I had to do was pretend that we . . . you know." She seemed embarrassed, unable to say anything more explicit. "She wanted your wife to see me. But then she told me she wouldn't pay me until I let everyone know you were my protector and wrote to your wife, telling her that we were lovers."

James' rage was rising again with each word this woman spoke. How could a mother do something like that to her own son?

"Why have you had a change of heart now?"

More tears streamed down the young woman's face. "Lady Raine hasn't given me the money she promised, and my son is sick. I . . . I can't lose him."

Although he did not agree with Miss Proust's actions, he understood her desperation. He would do anything to protect his siblings and their children. They lived in a cruel world where one's birth quite frequently dictated the course of their entire life without the hope of advancing.

"I just want to make things right, Lord Raine."

So did he.

WITH MISS PROUST on her way to her son with the funds his mother had promised and a written confession from her in his pocket, he went to confront his mother.

He was still in disbelief over her actions. How could she hate Evelina enough to destroy his marriage, his happiness? This went far beyond simple dislike or a clash of personalities. And what else had she done out of hatred and spite?

She did not turn as he entered the room, but kept her gaze centered on the window, her back rigid.

"Why do you detest Evelina?"

He wasn't expecting her to answer so promptly, but when she did, her tone was matter of fact, devoid of any emotion. "She aided Daisy in marrying far beneath her station. She encourages young ladies of the *ton* to act on desire rather than duty."

"Evelina has been nothing but dutiful since our marriage!"

"At what cost to this family?" She still had not looked his way. "That family has courted scandal for far too long. They deserve the *ton*'s scorn and disapproval."

James was about to argue that both Evelina's sisters had made excellent matches when something odd struck him about her words. "What do you mean 'courted scandal for too long?'"

"Nothing." Mother waved a hand in dismissal. "I'm tired. Let me alone."

James crossed the room and stood in front of where she was standing, but she continued to keep her gaze focused on the window. Crossing his arms, he said, "I can wait here all night until I discover the truth and the true source of your anger."

For the second time in only a few minutes, his mother surprised him with a prompt answer. "Do you think I wanted to be your father's second choice for a bride after Miss Summerford refused him? Do you think I enjoyed how he kept pining away for her year after year even after she married Lord Grace? Or how he kept a locket with her hair close to his heart? Or how he constantly reminded me that I was not her?"

Shock rendered him momentarily speechless. He knew his parents hadn't married for love, but hearing that his father had formed an earlier attachment to Evelina's mother was the last thing he'd ever expected. Shock gave way to disgust. "So because of his actions, you thought to destroy my happiness with Evelina?"

Mother gave a slight shrug of her shoulder. "From the moment you met her, you've changed. She would only have contributed to your downfall, just like *that woman* did with your father. The gossip and rumors, the sleeping aid in the decanter in your study, Miss Proust . . . they were all necessary means to an end."

His mother was behind the vicious gossip, drugging him, trying to destroy his world, his marriage, all because she sought revenge. He finally had the answers he'd been searching out for months.

"Yes, it is true. I have changed." For the first time since he'd entered the room, his mother looked at him. The expression on her face was self-satisfied, as if this admission justified her behavior. "I've changed for the better," his statement was firm, absolute. She looked away. "Evelina has made me want to be a better man, to be a husband in every sense of the word. She has taught me what it is like to want to do better, be better. She has taught me to love."

*Love.*

He was in love with his wife. The thought did not scare him, quite the contrary. His heart soared with the sudden knowledge that he was in love with Evelina.

That was all that mattered. He was done wasting his time in his mother's presence. She would not change. She would hold on to the bitterness that had been consuming her life until the day she drew her last breath. The only pleasure she'd found in life was making others miserable. He was not going to let her bitterness destroy the one thing that mattered most in his life.

"You may reside here in London, but if you breathe even the tiniest whisper against Evelina or anyone in her family again, I will ensure that you spend the rest of your days in the darkest corner of England." And with that, he took his leave and never looked back.

# Chapter Eighteen

A FTER ALL THE revelations that had come to light in the past hour, James wanted nothing more than to leave London and go to his wife immediately. But duty called. The Season was nearing its end and Jessica was on the brink of a proposal. He would not abandon her to the likes of his mother. He hoped Henrietta would be up for the challenge of chaperoning. If not . . .

"Good afternoon, Lord Raine," Martin said as he entered. "Your sister is awaiting your return in the study."

"Thank you, Martin." James was not a man of many words, but he appreciated his staff and their loyalty, never more so than now. "And thank you for being so diligent in your duties and letting me know about the letter my mother confiscated."

"Lady Raine—your wife, that is—is truly a remarkable woman and one that we all would protect." It appeared that James wasn't the only one in awe of Evelina.

"I appreciate that, Martin. I will go see my sister."

With a nod of his head, the efficient butler went about his duties. James would see to it that his entire staff received a well-deserved bonus.

James had only taken one step into the room when his sister began to speak in a hushed tone so as to not wake the sleeping toddler in her arms. "Martin said you went to see Mother. What did you discover?"

"She was the source of the gossip this Season and hired a Miss Proust to sleep in my bed in the hope that Evelina would find us together." It was still hard to believe his own mother would stoop to such an extreme low all in the name of revenge that had nothing to do with anyone living.

"Do you know where to find this Miss Proust?"

He rubbed his tired eyes. "She showed up while I was at Mother's and confessed everything. The woman was desperate for money to aid her sick child, and that's why she did what she did."

"I can understand that." Henrietta held her son a little closer to her heart and in that moment, James understood better a mother's desperation to protect her child. If he had any doubts about allowing Miss Proust to leave his mother's home unimpeded, they completely diminished in that moment. "Where is Miss Proust now?"

"I paid her the money Mother promised, plus more to start a new life away from Town. And in return, she wrote a letter to Evelina explaining her role in the subterfuge." James only hoped it was enough to win his wife back.

"I hope Miss Proust and her child will be all right." There was a softness to Henrietta's tone that he'd never heard before.

"I believe they will be."

It felt good to help those in need. He wished the course of events had been different, but he could not change the past. He knew now without even a whisper of doubt that he'd been faithful to his wife and that what happened was part of his mother's schemes. Next he intended to set things right. Hopefully it was not too late.

"I still cannot fathom why Mother did what she did. How could any mother stir such gossip against her child, regardless of age?" Henrietta marveled.

James then told Henrietta all that he'd learned that afternoon about their parents, and when he was done, the only question she had was, "Did you discover anything about Evelina?"

"She's with her sisters at Blackburn Hall, but—"

"You needn't worry. I'll chaperone Jessica. I suspect Mr. Drinkwater will officially offer for her quite soon," she offered with a sincere smile. "You go to Evelina. I suspect she's hurting just as much as you are."

It warmed his heart to know that his sister cared for his wife, too. With the recent turn of events, he suspected much change was on the horizon for his family, perhaps even a closeness with his own siblings he'd seldom hoped for. And he owed it all to Evelina.

James went to his elder sister and kissed her on the cheek. "Thank you."

JAMES DID NOT waste another moment. After instructing his valet on what he required, he packed a small traveling valise and went to retrieve his horse. Hermes was the fastest horse he'd ever owned and was without a doubt up for the challenge of getting him to Blackburn Hall post-haste.

Once Hermes was saddled, James left London, sweeping through the countryside as fast as his horse could travel, only stopping when they needed rest. Mile after mile, night after night, all he could think about was being reunited with Evelina, praying that she would forgive him.

By the time he'd reached the last inn, James was exhausted down to his bones. Tomorrow was the day he'd set things to rights. After a simple supper he retired, hoping sleep would not evade him again.

In the quiet of his room, thoughts of his time with Evelina played over and over in his mind. He missed the quiet evenings they'd spent in their residence, dancing, talking, learning about one another. He missed the sensual kisses and intoxicating looks she gave. He even missed the poetry books stacked by her bedside. More than anything, he just missed her.

What he'd told his mother was true. Evelina made him want to be a better man, but even more important, a better husband. Years ago, he'd vowed to himself that he would not become like his father—keeping mistress after mistress, lying to get what he wanted, and overall, being an unpleasant man.

But now, it simply was not enough to just avoid becoming like him. He wanted to rise above all the gossip and not only prove the naysayers wrong, but also prove to himself and his wife that he was worthy. Worthy of her love. Worthy of being her husband. Just worthy.

As he stared up at the dark ceiling, he said a silent prayer. He prayed that Evelina would forgive him, but he also gave thanks for the love he'd discovered. Soon, his eyelids grew heavy and he drifted off to sleep. It was the sleep his mind and body desperately needed.

The next morning, a serene calm washed over him as he started the last leg of his journey. Today was the day he would declare his love for his wife.

As he rode ever closer, however, that calm mixed with excitement and nervous tension. How could so many conflicting emotions roil within all at the same time?

How would Evelina react when she saw him? Would she let him explain? Would she yell and scream, full of dramatics like his mother? Or worse, would she remain silent?

James thought he could handle any reaction save silence.

Over the many miles covered, he'd rehearsed a speech, but as Blackburn Hall came into view, all those words disappeared. *Speak from the heart.*

Wasting no time, James charged up the front steps. Too much time had passed since he'd seen his wife. As soon as he entered the grand hall he was greeted by His Grace, the Duke of Blackburn.

"I see you received my letter," Niall said, his tone—

surprisingly—holding no hostility.

"I almost didn't." Frustration and anger over his mother's actions still burned in his chest. "My mother intercepted the letter, but my butler informed me of what had occurred and I confronted her."

"Why would she take the letter?"

Before he had a chance to answer, Alexandra, followed by the youngest Grace sister, Theodora, walked into the hall arm in arm. He suspected when any of these sisters joined together, they were a true force to be reckoned with.

"Who took what letter and for what purpose?" Alexandra questioned as she eyed James, most likely to assess whether he would lie.

"My mother took the letter the duke sent me. She was behind the gossip in Town . . . all of it. She also had me drugged and paid a courtesan to sleep in my bed."

"And why should we believe you after the hell you dragged our sister through?" Theodora's fiery words echoed off the crème and white marble of the hall.

"Theodora, please," Alexandra begged in a soothing tone. "Perhaps we should—"

"I have Miss Proust's confession here," he said as he pulled the letter from his pocket. "Although not proud of her actions, she was a victim in my mother's schemes as well."

Just then, Damian, the Earl of Grimsby, strolled into the room. He looked different from the last time James had seen him, and then he realized he was sans mask. His scars—James was glad to see—were hardly noticeable.

"My wife is rather passionate when it comes to her sisters," the large man teased as he moved closer to James. He pointed to the letter in his hand. "May I?"

It appeared that James would have to prove his innocence to almost every member of Evelina's family before he could see her. This was not how he imagined their reunion, but he would do whatever was required.

No sooner had James handed the letter to Damian, then the butler entered and announced, "Lady Middleton's carriage has just arrived."

The two sisters present looked at each other with surprise, then Alexandra turned to her husband, who answered her unspoken question. "Before I sent word to James, I sent a letter to your aunt, inviting her here. I thought she should be present when we discovered the truth."

James rolled his eyes heavenward. *Give me strength.*

"I came as soon as I received your letter," Lady Middleton said as she swept into the room and straight to her nieces. After several hugs, the older woman looked to Niall. "What did I miss?"

"James was confessing."

"He has nothing to confess. It was all his mother's doing," Lady Middleton defended. Wide, shocked eyes went from James to the older woman. "I have my own sources, and they are quite reliable and efficient." She removed her gloves, finger by finger, as she continued to explain. "When Evelina came to me, I decided to take investigative matters into my own hands. It would seem Miss Proust has a very powerful admirer who had only just been able to discover the source of his beloved's recent distress when I spoke with him. And it turns out he did not care for the elder Lady Raine's actions. He was happy to make the whole truth known to me, and I believe he intends to offer for the woman. I daresay she will accept." She then turned and addressed James. "Oh, and by the way, Mr. Drinkwater will be offering for Jessica as soon as he's able to speak with her father. And she intends to accept him."

At least that was one less worry.

James had missed much as he wallowed in his despair for a week. If he'd had his wits about him, he'd have gone to Lady Middleton first. "Who's the gentleman that Miss Proust—"

"Some wealthy Spanish merchant," Lady Middleton said with a wave of her hand as if it were every day that a courtesan caught the attention of a wealthy man and then was offered marriage and security.

Voices swirled through the hall, each with a different theory as to why his mother acted the way she had, but in the end, they all seemed pleased that James was innocent in the scheme that was not of his doing. For once.

The truth was out, and still James had yet to see his wife. The one woman he wanted to see and apologize to was hidden somewhere within this pile of bricks and he was practically being held captive by her family. He could not take another second of waiting.

"May I please see my wife now?" his loud voice broke through the chaos.

Two sisters-in-law, two husbands, and one great-aunt stared at him, contemplating his request. Silence reigned for several seconds until the sweetest, most seductive voice he'd ever heard drifted through the hall and into his heart.

"I would like a moment alone with Lord Raine." He turned and saw his heart's desire descending the stairs. *Evelina.*

Had she said "a moment?" James didn't want just *a moment.* He wanted a lifetime. And *Lord Raine?* Well, at least she had acknowledged his presence.

Evelina did not wait for anyone to answer but turned and walked away. Without question, James followed. He would follow her to the ends of the earth and back if that was what it took to prove his love for her.

James followed her to a small sunlit drawing room. Rich hues of green and blue filled the room, easing the tension. She went to a chair beside the fireplace. Soft, soothing warmth drifted outward into the room. He didn't know whether to take a seat beside her or across from her, to stand or kneel and beg forgiveness. In the end, he decided to sit across from her.

She didn't speak, which suited James. He had much to say and wanted to be able to get it all out at once, but didn't know where to start just the same.

*Speak from the heart.*

"I did not dishonor our vows. I never invited another woman to my bed, nor will I ever. My mother paid a courtesan to be in my bed, to pretend we slept together. Mother was the one at the source of the constant rumors this Season and has been dealt with accordingly. You will never have to interact with her again, nor will she again spew such vitriol toward you or anyone in your family." James stood and started to pace, too nervous to sit still. There was much at stake. "From the moment I saw you, I knew you were the only woman for me. Wanting you . . ." He turned to face her. "Wanting you to be my wife had nothing to do with begetting an heir. All those months ago when I said you seduced me, I meant it. I have thoughts of no other woman, no desire to be near another. I think I fell in love with you the moment I saw you. Evelina, I am yours."

One moment, Evelina was sitting perfectly still listening to him, and in the next, she burst into tears. No, not tears, but a loud uncontrollable sob. Her shoulders shook with great force, ripping through James. He went to her and knelt in front of her.

James cradled her face with a gentle hand. "I never meant to cause you such pain."

Her sobs eased and then the soft words drifted from her beautiful mouth on a whisper, "You . . . you love me?"

Their eyes locked as their breaths came in unison. "With all my heart, more than life itself. I love you, Evelina." He then pressed his lips to hers, caressing her mouth, sealing his vow with a kiss.

Slowly the kiss ended, and she pulled back. "I blamed you for this marriage, *Lord Raine*," she teased with a seductive half-smile that sent his pulse racing. "But I think I fell head over heels the moment I saw you, too."

"Evelina, you are without a doubt the most stubborn, passionate, caring, intelligent woman I have ever met. And I adore you." He moved his mouth over hers, devouring its softness, enjoying the feel of her lips against his. He would never tire of kissing his wife. He rested his forehead against hers. "I may not be the poet your heart desired, but I have been trying to be more poetic in my words." James took a small, folded note from his pocket and handed it to his wife. "I wrote this for you."

Evelina took the note and read aloud. "All the days I've spent surrounded by peers, but felt alone, all the duels I've fought, but without true purpose, all the lips I've kissed, but never loved, have brought me to you." She leaned in and brushed a kiss to his lips. "This . . . it's beautiful."

Her eyes filled with tears as her gentle gaze caressed his soul, and James knew that whatever tribulations came their way, they would survive because they loved each other with a desire and passion that was once in a lifetime.

# Epilogue

*Nine months later*

J AMES PACED DOWN the hall outside the viscountess' suite for what felt like the thousandth time.

"You've got to calm down," Niall implored. "The women have it under control, I am certain. You just need to—"

"I can't calm down! It has been nearly twenty hours and—"

*Oh! Owww!* A loud scream rattled the closed bedroom door.

Pain and helplessness made his heart ache. How much longer could she endure? A dreadful thought occurred to him.

*What if Evelina did not survive?*

No. He could not lose her, not now, not ever. James had never been the praying kind, not until he'd nearly lost Evelina once before. But once again, he sent a prayer heavenward, hoping it would be answered. *Please let her survive.*

Another scream pierced the walls. James took in a long, shaky breath attempting to be calm, attempting not to think about all that could go wrong. He began pacing the floor once again, ignoring the exhaustion consuming him. He would not rest until he knew his wife was safely delivered of their child.

Both Niall and Damian had been by his side since the labor began and both had tried to comfort him as the minutes turned into hours, fusing together in one long agonizing moment.

Maids rushed in and out of the room, but there was still no

word on Evelina, just reassurances that all was as it should be, which did nothing to ease his anxiety.

More agonizing minutes dragged on, clawing at his happiness as thoughts of never seeing his wife again ravaged his mind.

"That's it," James said as he rushed toward the door. Niall's distant words of reassurance fading as he opened the door and was met with the sound of a different sort of cry.

He stopped in his tracks. Slow, easy breaths filled his lungs as he saw the woman he loved, clearly exhausted, but alive. Alive and smiling. Smiling and holding a small bundle. And still James could not move.

"Congratulations, Lord Raine," the accoucheur said.

Alexandra wiped damp strands of hair from Evelina's face, then kissed her cheek. "You did beautifully, dearest."

Theodora kissed the other cheek. "We will give you some time alone." As she passed James, she offered a bright, encouraging smile.

A moment later, James and Evelina were alone.

"Are you feeling all right?" he said, unsure what to say as he approached the bed.

"Better than all right." Her smile was one of serene bliss. "Would you like to meet your son?"

"I have a son?" he whispered as he neared, then sat on the edge of the bed.

She simply nodded her head, and her smile filled his soul. He could not remember Evelina looking more beautiful than in that moment, holding their son.

"May . . . may I hold him?"

With great care, she handed him the tiny bundle. His son let out a wide yawn, revealing a matching set of dimples. He was absolute perfection.

James leaned in and brushed a kiss to Evelina's rosy cheek. "Thank you, my love."

"It looks like we both got what we wanted after all," Evelina said as she reached over to kiss their son, and then James.

# About the Author

Bestselling, award-winning author, Alanna Lucas pens Regency-set historicals filled with romance, adventure, and of course, happily ever afters. When she is not daydreaming of her next travel destination, Alanna can be found researching, spending time with family, tending to her garden, or going for long walks. She makes her home in California with her husband and children, and too many books to count.

Just for the record, you can never have too many handbags or books. And travel is a must.